MARTHA LUISA HERNÁNDEZ CADENAS (Guantánamo, 1991) is a playwright, writer, and performer. She studied Theater Studies at the University of the Arts, ISA. She has published the poetry collections *Días de hormigas* (Ediciones Unión, 2018), which won the 2017 David Poetry Prize, *Los vegueros* (Sureditores Collection, 2019) and *El Palacio de las Ursulinas* (Ediciones La Luz, 2021), and in 2016 founded ediciones **sinsentido**. Her performance works include *Nueve* (2017), *No soy unicornio* (2019) – which received the ZKB Acknowledgement Prize at the 2022 Zürcher Theater Spektakel – and *Escribir con la lengua* (2022). Her work has been presented in Colombia, Argentina, Chile, Mexico, Spain, Germany, Canada and Switzerland. *The Weasel and the Whore* won the 2020 Franz Kafka Prize.

JULIA SANCHES is a translator from Portuguese, Spanish, and Catalan. Recent translations include *Living Things* by Munir Hachemi and *Mammoth* by Eva Baltasar, both longlisted for the Cercador Prize. Sanches was longlisted for the International Booker Prize 2025 for her co-translation of Dahlia de la Cerda's *Reservoir Bitches*.

JENNIFER SHYUE is a translator from Spanish. Her translations include Julia Wong Kcomt's poetry collections *A Blind Salmon* and *Vice-royal-ties*, as well as Augusto Higa Oshiro's novel *The Enlightenment of Katzuo Nakamatsu*, which received the ALTA First Translation Prize. She can be found at shyue.co.

MARTHA LUISA HERNÁNDEZ CADENAS

The Weasel and the Whore

Translated by
Julia Sanches and Jennifer Shyue

PRESS

First published in English in Great Britain in 2025 by
Héloïse Press Ltd
Canterbury
www.heloisepress.com

First published under the original Spanish language title *La puta y el hurón*
© Martha Luisa Hernández Cadenas, 2023

This translation © Julia Sanches and Jennifer Shyue, 2025

Edited by Saba Ahmed

Cover design by Laura Kloos

Text design and typesetting by Tetragon, London
Printed and bound in Great Britain by CPI Group (UK) Ltd, Croydon, CR0 4YY

The moral right of Martha Luisa Hernández Cadenas to be identified as the author of this work has been asserted in accordance with the Copyright, Designs and Patents Act 1988.

Julia Sanches and Jennifer Shyue assert their moral right to be identified as the translators of the work.

All rights reserved. Except as otherwise permitted under current legislation, no part of this publication may be reproduced or transmitted in any form or by any means, electronic or mechanical, including photocopy, recording, or any information storage and retrieval system, without permission in writing from the publisher.

This book has been selected to receive financial assistance from English PEN's PEN Translates programme, supported by Arts Council England. English PEN exists to promote literature and our understanding of it, to uphold writers' freedoms around the world, to campaign against the persecution and imprisonment of writers for stating their views, and to promote the friendly co-operation of writers and the free exchange of ideas. www.englishpen.org.

ISBN 978-1-7384594-5-2

This book is a work of fiction. Any resemblance to names, characters, organisations, places and events is entirely coincidental.

EU GPSR Authorised Representative
LOGOS EUROPE, 9 rue Nicolas Poussin, 17000, LA ROCHELLE, France
e-mail: contact@logoseurope.eu

To Rogelio.
To Celia.
To Joanna.

[…] the soul of the little girl is like a rosebud shrouded in crepe, a bunch of violets dimming in the snow, a disk of stars sunk in a murky lake.

JULIÁN DEL CASAL, "JUANA BORRERO"

I'm forgetting how alcohol feels in my body, how a dick feels in my body, how feeling love feels in my body. Yes, I'm forgetting it all.

ROGELIO ORIZONDO, *GIRLS*

Dear Mary,

I always thought we'd stay friends after the cataclysm, but nothing happened the way we planned. Look at me now, throwing money away and surviving, walking long distances and going the wrong direction on the metro. Daily life defined by cents, sustenance, bodies. In this unchanging routine I almost never write, or I write very little, which is how writing became more of a need than a narcissistic practice. I left behind my self-absorbed way of writing the afternoon I thought I was about to get locked away for years. I turned my back on everything tying me to that country and to you. I didn't think I could manage another night in jail. Those two nights I'd spent at a police station in Centro Habana were still fresh in my mind.

I usually sit at Le Relais de Belleville. Once or twice a week, I come here and pretend to talk to you. Maybe pretend isn't the right word because I really do talk to you, I share a bit of news, I tell you about the underwear I'm wearing, my cotton sheets, or soy milk, the only kind of milk I can drink.

I imagine you're doing alright. Even though you acted like you were fragile and self-destructive, you were always fine, you could always complain because you had a good mother. Please give her a hug, tell her I rewrote her story, which I had to change because I could no longer remember her face. Your features are out of focus now too, how could I try to preserve them in my head when they were already gone.

Over the years, I've become a big fan of insects. They're drawn to rot. I used to think it was insects that made things decay. I talked about Cuba as a place of infection. If I'm writing you this letter, it's because I've changed my mind. I don't regret what we lived through, but I do regret not knowing how to live through it better. You know it couldn't have happened any other way, because we were happy in that trash heap where we were in love with tramps. We were like lonely little bumblebees scared away by Cuban society. Society is so scary.

Why bother writing about my first days in Europe, the life I used to have with Gérard, those years were a wash: I was his third-world whore, his special Cubanita, his Caribbean oddity. After Gérard, I was with a guy ten years younger than me. I still find myself unable to describe the love I felt for him. He wanted kids, so we tried to adopt or pay for a surrogate. Everything went wrong.

Then the guy who was ten years younger than me left me for someone his own age. We met my replacement at a club together, and I don't know how, but I could sense what would happen from the way they pretended not to look at each other. I could tell you about us, about the mole on his lower lip or how I liked to spy on him as he slept, when he showered, as he left work and took the metro. I liked that in my head he was like a stranger and it was like our life together was a figment of my playwright's imagination, it was as if I was even more anonymous than I already am as an immigrant, as if my existence depended on him, it was no longer real.

I'm starting to feel old. I'm starting to feel kind of deaf, like I can't write what I hear anymore because my hearing is failing and writing is about listening carefully, though that's a cliché, and it only works because I'm out of ideas. Writing gives me ideas. Writing everyday trivial things helps me with the traumas I dragged in from our putrid place of origin.

The first thing you forget is the voice. I have videos where we're naked and acting drunk, I have this one of you singing and reading poems from the notebook we found at Coppelia that we never managed to get back to its owner, but I've forgotten your voice because the videos don't sound like you, I can tell you don't actually sound like that because I don't either. That's not your face. Or your body. But most of all, it's not your voice.

On the weekends I go to the country to be with a much older Italian man, a chef from the south of Italy. We've realized that Sunday melts away when you walk on grass. He grows his own food and shows me all the effort that goes into the details, with him I can savor an unshakeable calm that sits outside of time, and I let myself be carried away.

My Italian lover makes me feel desired like I've never felt before. When he's inside me, everything feels at peace, as if he were filling an inexplicable emptiness, and I want him to push into me in that real, old-fashioned way.

We were allergic to being still. I would've loved you, I swear, I would've, but I don't want to see what you've turned into, I don't want to know that you're alive and happy, I'm not interested in knowing about you, not really, I'd rather come to the café and talk to you in my imagination about the American company where my job is to answer messages in Spanish. Boring, right?

I have no idea if you're still in theater, still doing set design, if you write poetry, if you like getting ice cream to soften the edges of your invalidity, if you've gotten rid of that stink in your armpits. We were invalids, we were unhappy, we were childish, and we had something that couldn't be taken from us: For us, the world lasted a few seconds at a time, reality was orgasmic, our decisions were totally off the mark, and nothing changed. We spent our days wallowing in the pigsty, we expected the worst, because the worst was the only true thing.

We were bigger idiots than the insects, and there's nothing more idiotic than an insect in Cuba. I feel bad for insects because they're carrion-eaters, and you and I never were, though I guess who isn't, at least a little. You know what I'm talking about, I'm talking about that carrion feeling, it was the same no matter if we went forward or back because there was no future and no past.

I smoke a lot of weed here, but it's good stuff, what we used to smoke was poison, it always made us dizzy, more stupid. Maybe you don't live there anymore, maybe you've gone vegan. Something tells me you've gained a lot more weight and don't remember how we loved each other. I'm thinking you haven't had kids either. I bet you'll stay single and keep believing it's worth it to make theater and look idealistically at art. You haven't learned to listen. And sometimes it's important to be one giant ear.

What hurts the most about not knowing anything about you is the feeling that what happened to us never actually happened, that it won't ever happen or be experienced by us again. I'm left with this huge emptiness. Cuba is you, it was me and you in that pit, we were the plague. Here, everyone thinks that Cuba is Fidel Castro. But they're so wrong...

That play I wrote for your mother ended like this, remember?

ANTI-VECTOR SUPERWOMAN says:

I want to kill you, motherfuckers, milk-white motherfuckers, I want to kill you all and never see you again. For there to be nothing left of you on this earth, you milquetoast motherfuckers. For none of your infectious milk to fall on this earth. For none of your polluting milk to fall on our sovereign soil. For none of your children to fall upon our rivers. Wherever a single mosquito of you lands, there I'll be; wherever you can be exterminated, there I'll be. I want there to be no trace of your reek, for you to not come steal our children, or try to harm our revolutionary morale with your crappy soft-porn ideology. Go shit out flies, pigs, fags, degenerates. You'll have to get past me.

[Hundreds of gigantic *Aedes aegypti* mosquitoes circle closer to Anti-Vector Superwoman. She kills them all. Her daughter closes her eyes. She was not born to defend the fatherland from pests.]

How's your mother? Sometimes I remember her convulsing, falling, and wonder if she's still having seizures. I hope not.
Love you, Pamela

CONVULSION

My mother is on the floor. Muscles tensed. Arteries contracted. A trickle of blood. Drool. Eyes rolled back. Fingers curled. My mother is on the bed. The needle is in my hand. I inject her, and my eyes well up.

It isn't Sunday for the Defense or any other day of patriotic volunteerism, it's the Saturday after his death. The house is quiet. The streets are on mute. He died last night, and the hallway where my mother, my sister, and I live has been seized by a strange sense of peace. I say Fidel Castro is dead, and this fact doesn't shatter the calm that lies between the wall, Sunday, my right arm, the gelatinous immanence of mourning, and my mother.

Yesterday, as I was dancing at the party for the Muestra de Cine Joven film festival, the news of his death seemed like a tired, unoriginal joke. I picture my mother trying to watch an action movie while nursing a headache. I picture us bopping around at the party. Nothing can stop her from moving: she sweats, drools, is born, epilepsy is a state of mind the way death is a musical happening.

It's Saturday and my mother is in my arms, the only ritual I can't escape. There's a bruise on my arm, the one supporting her hot neck, which is a vessel of fear and the collapse of her healthy mind. What is a healthy mind? Does it heal? Help? Is it alive? Is she dreaming of a bearded man who promises to take care of her? Of a revolution that goes off like a camera flash when we dance? Of my birth?

He pulled me into the bathroom at the party and grabbed me so hard my blood reversed course. I laughed off the ache, acted like the bruise had meaning, a hidden meaning that had nothing to do with violence or fragility but with loss. Lost, I fell, I fell in that bathroom like my mother's skull hitting the floor. It's so easy to be broken skin in a stranger's intensity. . .

With the news swirling and my mother in my arms, I think about the needle and the crumbling of the hallway, and I breathe in the air exhaled by this block, this street, this city, this province, a country as muted as me in a shadowy bathroom, a Revolution that's actually a body letting itself be dragged and manipulated like a puppet that longs to be animated by joy. The unseen joy of those of us who were given a sentimental socialist education: "Pioneers for communism." The only thing to breathe in this place is the uneasiness of death and failure: "Venceremos." We will overcome. But not everything is that loathing: "Vamos bien." We're doing fine.

It's Saturday, a damp Saturday, and the atmosphere is heavy with a certain monstrousness. One by one the weasels come into the hallway to gather signatures, to tell me to leave, to announce they have something to show me. The weasels don't notice my mother suffering in my arms, or my hematoma (by force of blood pooling and complacent sex), the weasels judge my mother's insignificance and my own. In a little room in Centro Habana, my mother and I are like prayer cards of terror, of the eternal fall and incurable illness. My mother and I, with our own private Committee for the Defense of the Revolution-style choreography, a choreography oblivious to its place in the current historic moment.

My cellphone rang, my mother fell, my sister said: "Mamá fell." I ran out of the party right as we were getting the news that some people celebrated with their hips, their knees, their asses swaying on the floor. I ran out of there to save my mother.

Fidel is a portrait or an idea (I can't make up my mind); my mother is a belly button and long fingers untangling my hair.

My mother had her first epileptic seizure after giving birth to my sister sixteen years ago. She's gotten every diagnosis: claustrophobia, hysteria, manic depression, words that point to an invisible epileptic focus no exam can pick up, a mystery that entertains doctors and inspires all sorts of notions and root causes.

There's no evidence of illness, just an echoing in her body—so old, dejected, vanquished, my mother's jelly brain and jelly mouth. She's evidence of the flaws in the clinical frameworks that have yet to take hold in this country, and of its deadening soul. This day is jelly, like my mother's brain after a seizure.

When my sister says, "Mamá fell," she and I are the only ones in the whole nation who are truly sad.

For the past sixteen years, my mother has taken pills that don't help manage the seizures or the contortions, how she dies for a few seconds at a time. Sheet and floor bloodied, head broken into a thousand pieces, brain and teeth pocked with holes, teeth falling out as her head smashes into the toilet bowl, the sink, the cold tile; the open fridge, empty, littered with leftovers, my mother's body a mannequin dripping blood inside a fridge, a mannequin pretending to pose for a mundane advertisement.

An extraordinary Saturday that passes slowly, teeming with weasels—all male—who make an unnecessary amount of noise and repeat unnecessary slogans. I'd like to take a portrait of her lying in my arms, of her mouth that seems to speak through my blurred, maudlin bruise, the imprint of a stupid fumble in the bathroom.

I want to take a photo of her, and out come ulcers, tatagua butterflies, insects, stammered lines around her cheekbones and eyebrows, out comes this urge to write her, to enter her body after a convulsion. There is no grief as glorious as looking at my mother and knowing that Fidel's death means nothing.

Hair. Pores. Long nose. Full lips. Rounded cheekbones. She asks for juice. For water. I moisten her lips. She complains I did a lousy job injecting her. Foam. Let's go to the beach. Let's go dancing. Let's celebrate this Saturday. My sister says, "Mamá fell," and Mamá laughs and laughs. She's never happy around me, but she laughs.

National mourning: disciplining the body, playing with paper dolls, throwing eggs, printing books for higher education, making models for my seminar in set design. *You're a naughty girl, get a grip.* Wearing glasses and picking fleas off my left foot's little toe, plucking ticks from the soft fuzz on my friend Pamela's face. I've changed myself just enough to become a pubescent artist, a woman who renounces any and all official and political acts, a naughty girl who doesn't meet expectations, an addict to political incorrectness. It's not my thing, I'm not interested, it doesn't affect me, doesn't feed me. This is what people call a dry law. In the meantime, sad thoughts, achingly sad thoughts.

My grandfather died on a hot afternoon. The sky was hellishly overexposed, and I was at school at ISA, the Instituto Superior de Arte, with my friend E. We wanted someone to write us a letter of invitation so we could go to Argentina, and we were composing long emails to that effect.

We counted the slats in the shutters and played footsie while E wrote down what I said: "We are young artists in the field of set design and performance theater." I remember we were trying to finish a scale model made of recycled cans, but that was later. The only thing I know for sure is that we sat there wanting to travel while the heat and bright sunlight slipped through the grant's window of opportunity.

My phone rang—it was my aunt telling me my grandfather had died.

I cried all the way to her house, and when I got there everyone was quiet. I went up to his bed and held him, and my grandfather's body held me, and it felt like we were commemorating something above and beyond our lives. His body seemed alive, hazily alive but still alive, and my first impulse was to lie down beside him. Everyone got upset. My aunt regretted calling me.

"She's an artist. That's why she has to be the center of attention," they said. "She's an idiot." My father wasn't around to see it. My father hasn't been around for a long time.

My aunt slapped me. Who did I think I was, holding my grandfather to my chest, what was I trying to prove. Such a heroic gesture from a granddaughter swanning in from university, her grandfather bedridden for a whole year while she dreamed of going to Argentina.

My grandfather is the only man I've ever loved. I can't stop thinking of him as a hellish abyss that burns my eyes. When I think of his body in the heat of every day, in my sweat and tears, I open my eyes to the fact that I am alone in his memory, in death.

My grandfather's death is the only death. There is no sadder thought than the thought of his death.

I'm scheduled to go to R's house today. I have no idea what state the old man will be in, but I bet he won't want to do anything—the country is in mourning, and he's probably self-flagellating like the illustrious weasel he is. I hope he just wants to talk.

There's third-world melancholy concentrated in the mustiness of R's breath, which sprays me in the face when he says my name:

    M
       A
          R
             Y

R is one of those men who feels the need to talk incessantly, as if they had real opinions. One of those men who likes to try to pay for car rides with twenty-dollar bills, then apologize and pull a ten-CUC note out of his overstuffed wallet, which the driver doesn't have change for either. At the end of this interaction, R will take out a ten-peso note, one he had all along and could've paid with from the beginning, but at least he got to show the other riders he's got cash and couldn't care less about the exchange rate.

The third world produces this kind of man, the weasel man.

I go to his house on Sundays, a routine athletic visit. He has a lot of money, a fortune that I'm sure comes from a misspent family inheritance and renting out a mansion in Varadero. I look at him and know exactly what he is: The man kept it all—the gold and riches passed down—and became a weasel. The male weasel is a rapist. He sinks his teeth into the female's neck when he thrusts into her, a natural part of animal mating.

R for Repulsion. R for Revolution. R for routine rage rude rune runt rare renegade redick refuck redeath.

I knock on the front door. He opens with unusual glee. I don't understand why he's so cheerful.

"You're here early. . ."

"His death didn't give you a heart attack?"

"Come in."

"Are you in mourning?"

"How's your mother doing?"

I don't answer. Not unless I want to. We have an agreement and that's sacred, an agreement between the two of us, which makes it no less disgusting or absurd.

My mother met him at his house during her campaign. The campaign had to do with mosquitoes and job opportunities for people like my mother, who doesn't have a degree.

The first offer he made was to her, because my mother is a beautiful woman any man would desire: She'd come over once or twice a week to keep him company.

R was moved from the start by my family's financial situation. Soon he began taking it upon himself to invite us over for long lunches at his two-story property. I could tell what he wanted the moment I looked him in the eyes. If I have any talent at all, it has to be this, knowing what people want from me. One look, and I know. Then R made my mother a second offer. A different offer.

We sit down at the table. He's talking about a script he's writing or a novel he wrote or storylines that are a dime a dozen in the world of fiction and the world of actual facts. He's going on about a string of stupid things I can't stand. At my age I'm so intolerant I can't even stand myself.

Sometimes I enjoy this first moment of formality for the polite conversation that makes our relationship seem like an honest one. What happens then is simple, quick. The disgust comes before and after.

He serves me the bitter tea. I go to sleep. When I wake up, I'm in his room, half-naked and very dizzy. R carries out his weaselly rituals—talking, drugging me, leaving me thirty CUC, sometimes twenty, depending on his mood, under the pretty lamp on the dresser. I bet he enjoys watching me leave on shaky legs without saying goodbye while he smokes a Cuban cigar out on his terrace, under a sun hot enough to set fire to his tobacco and his black horn-rimmed glasses. He doesn't look at me or say anything, and I do my best to leave and not spend the rest of the day thinking about that snapshot on the terrace.

I can't figure out any other way of recounting what happens after we sit down at the table. It goes by in a breath, dissolves.

He sets me on my knees. Sticks a freezing piece of metal in me. Squeezes my breasts. Sucks on my neck. Puts a needle through my ear. Penetrates me deeply. Sticks his hand slick with pungent oil, Vaseline, and lube up into me until he feels something break, is thrilled at the breaking. Squeezes my hands. Ties me to the bed and smacks me in the face. Cries into my belly button. Scratches the palm of my hand with a wire brush. Spits on me. Pisses on me. Shaves off my eyebrows. Mocks me. Breaks cups over my knees. One over each knee. Screams at me. Sometimes he gives me a gentle kiss. Sometimes he whispers something in another language, utters a sentence in bad French: *Je vais encourir bien des reproches. Mais qu' y puis-je?* Sometimes he fishes out his intestines and carefully makes me swallow them. As he comes in my ear, puts his old-man milk in my ears, I am a dead woman.

All this could be happening and I wouldn't know.

We sit down at the table and I drink the tea. The weasel decides on the facts—after that point, it's possible the facts no longer exist. It wasn't like this on my first visit, or my second. On my third visit, we kissed, but my disgust was obvious, so he suggested I drink the tea, which I did because I wanted to disappear.

Four hours. Between the tea and the thirty CUC in my hand are three or four hours. I press record on my phone and it captures nothing but a wail, like the sound of a ram being slaughtered in cold blood. The sound frightens me. I have hours and hours of recordings. I should be scared, but I feel nothing. In the same way I've stopped being disgusted by his breath, I've stopped feeling. I'm a female weasel: even when I faint, I endure.

I thought R would be in mourning, but Fidel's death doesn't matter to him either, even though his endorsements would suggest otherwise.

R: I hope you die slowly, and your skin droops off your face like melting gum, and you stop being able to feel desire because desire doesn't want to be felt by you. I made a drawing of you as a weasel. You're the most rotten of them all because you have no morals. One day I'm going to report you to the police. You and your shitty old face. You and your shitty old skin. Your smell that won't leave my neck. You think you have power over my body, but my body is desire, and it suffers because it isn't free. I know your idea of sovereignty means acting like you have power over a dead woman. But I'm not dead, I'm asleep.

Last night I dreamed about Alberto, who went to my high school. He isn't on my mind for any particular reason, I guess maybe I'm thinking about him because everything about him was a mystery and his body looked like mine.

One time in tenth grade, we made out and groped each other by the sports fields of our residential high school, leaving damp like animals. Afterward, we laughed about that silly night, remembering the time we fooled around to break out of our boredom.

One Friday we didn't have class, they found Alberto in the bathroom. A gang of the school's heartthrobs and weasel machos walked in, and there was Alberto, much happier than he'd been with me, pressed up against another boy I don't really remember. They nearly beat him to death. I remember them bringing him out bathed in blood, and people shouting and opening up a space in the middle of the school's concrete central courtyard, which, thanks to the day off, looked like it was full of massive herds of animals emoting to the reggaeton of Elvis Manuel. The boy who'd been in the bathroom with Alberto was left alone—apparently he paid up. Alberto fell into the throng of people like a rabbit with its throat slit, and when I saw that horrifying scene, I took him to the infirmary with the help of two friends. The teachers, the biggest animals of them all, shit themselves laughing.

Alberto came back to school two weeks later. Every night he would open up his mouth in the bathroom, open up his ass, open up his head. They didn't hit him, just called him names in the central courtyard. A bunch of monsters shouting at him from the dorms as he left the dining hall, after making him swallow and swallow. They refused to say his name, as if that would protect them. Alberto was a rabbit drained of blood getting served up on a filthy cafeteria tray.

I remember one Sunday he didn't come outside. I also remember that the sports fields were like the Arctic Circle of Melena del Sur. I would sit there during every free period and try to remember the taste of Alberto's mouth. I think I wrote him a letter. You write letters to God to clear your conscience and letters to the dead as an act of rebellion. You write letters to friends to wash the fear from your body. Writing letters is the one thing that has saved me from feeling alone.

Alberto wasn't on any of the buses that pulled in that Sunday. He'd killed himself. Total silence. Alberto had been pushed to suicide. Nobody said anything except: "Revolution is a sense of the historical moment." I went to the sports fields to catch a cold and fell asleep from all the crying, my head against the concrete.

Alberto and my grandfather are always in my thoughts. They're the only people I wish I could've gotten to know better, the only people I wish I could spend Sundays with. I hate Sundays. There's no difference between these Sundays and Alberto's nights at school. Except for the fact that I'm a clown, a hunk of meat, and Alberto was a soul who couldn't be broken by semen, spit, or fists.

My mother's uniform is gray. For her job, she was given a black briefcase, a bag of Abate insecticide, two pamphlets about detecting and combating *Aedes aegypti* vectors, and a pair of orthopedic shoes. They also gave her liquid detergent, a thermometer for measuring the temperature of the water, a jar for taking samples of *Aedes aegypti* eggs, a mini-fumigator, a liquid for the mini-fumigator, and a blank form.

My mother relies on the thirty CUC we get from R. Her monthly salary of twenty-four CUC really isn't enough to fill our bellies. We have beef twice a week and smoked pork loin on Saturdays—she has a structured menu.

Forget the croquetas, hot dogs, and burgers, at home we live a life of dietary luxury thanks to the solidarity aid provided by R. My mother tells me my side job—that is, my Sunday visits—is the only thing I'm useful for. She doesn't say it out of malice but because she's washed her hands of the facts, she's drunk her own tea.

"I don't want to go anymore."

"Aren't you helping him with his papers, his research, the novel? I don't understand."

"Yup, that's totally what he does, talk to me about novels and literature."

"It's not like he's doing anything to you that you haven't already done. He's a man of the law. Look at everything he does for us. You're being ungrateful. What's he going to do, eat you?"

"Why don't you go?"

"Because you're the one who can help him with these things, what would I go for."

"You really are stupid, aren't you?"

"Watch your mouth. Go find yourself another job. Go study, or do a course. Do something. Don't bring me more problems or talk to me about things you don't understand. I'm not keeping a roof over your head only to sit here and swallow all your spite."

"It's all fucked."

"I don't know where you got that mouth of yours. Five years at university for this."

"Ay, Mami, zip it already."

"Zip it already, this is what I get for feeding you, for raising you and your sister by myself. You're a parasite, and while you live under my roof, you're going to watch what you say. You didn't learn any of that in this house."

On Sundays as the sun sets, I go for a walk, feeling weak, sad, detached, drugged out, I have no idea what R puts in his tea, I need to walk like I know where I'm going. I walk along the Malecón and look into people's eyes. I look inside their heads. I look through their throats. They walk shattered like me.

In my pocket are the thirty CUC R paid me. I buy an ice cream. People are distressed. The weasels are the most downcast, their eyes sad, their pupils sunken and dark with grief. Fidel died. His death has destabilized them, though that was also true of his birthday—people want justifications for their sadness or happiness because they don't know how to be happy. We're all the same. On this street, where I'm walking down with my ice cream, we're all equally wretched, we're broken in the same way, though I'm not thinking about Fidel, or about anything else.

It's the natural cycle of a depleted world, I guess, a universal feeling of melting and misfortune that has nothing to do with the privilege of holding an ice cream cone, but rather with death expanding, death in every place. All this death really makes me sad—the death of my country.

In this country, everyone is wearing a persona, either the persona anchored in pain and conviction or the one animated by bellyaching and rumba. These personas suffer from ancient enjoyment and have calluses on the bottoms of their feet. They've already metastasized, they've burned and plastered themselves onto the walls, sunk down, exploded, melted into nothing. But age-old things don't just fade into nothing, and neither does cancer—they're legendary experiences that survive everything. The persona in my head has really fucked-up logic.

What I do know is that when I look into people's eyes I see the virus, negation's source twisting in their throats,

I also see death, an inclination toward emptiness (not pure happiness or pure sadness but Cuban impurity, a legendary, carcinogenic impurity). That's what I see in people, in the weasels, in them, my pathetic reflections. Even as I regret investing in this ice cream cone that doesn't satisfy my every desire, I use logic to kill seconds, minutes, steps, blaring TVs and radios.

Today I'm going to spend this money on me or whoever else I want—it's mine, the results of my labor. I bring my phone to my ear and listen to the audio from this afternoon. The sounds I recorded in R's room help me know. I hear blows. I hear falling. I hear thudding, noises that wound.

This is the first time I'm hearing noises and not wails. Not the terror of a slaughtered ram, but me falling to the ground, against the headboard, someone else's voice coming out of me, and I can tell he likes it because he's moaning, crying, getting worked up. Weasels. Weasels walking, despite their grief, weasels wanting my skin.

My mother woke up feeling better. That's why she went and joined the committee the weasels put together to collect signatures of condolence. My mother, a woman undefeated. She does not remember her seizure, the bump on her head, her sore muscles, because there is something greater than her and her rest. My mother's only distinguishing feature is her plan to hand me over to R, though I guess it also makes sense that she's pressuring me into this revolutionary trade—to teach me a lesson, to help us survive.

The Cuban descendant of Italian businesspeople, R is a communist who stole everything he could from his family abroad. He writes scripts for the revolutionary cop shows on Cuban television. This is the biography of a big guy with military rank and caveats granted by the dominant patriarchal consciousness. This is R, a man who does what he wants.

I give myself to R as a way of complying with my mother's wishes, and I get paid for it (which satisfies my wishes too). Apparently, it's my duty as a lost young woman to contribute to the household with these pennies from our trades. Mission accomplished. At the end of the day, there's no evidence of what he's doing to me. Not even I could testify to what goes on in that room and to the noises made there. Mamá is of the opinion that I'm doing well to put my irrationality to use helping R with his writing. But I've never read anything by him or helped him beyond satiating his base impulses as a member of a semiviolent, semidomesticated species.

Today he briefly mentioned a Fidel biopic he plans to write.

He could've talked to my mother about that project.

I meet up with Pamela—my best friend, my playwright. She knows to kiss the back of my neck and sing me songs from her unreleased album *Elephant Family*. Track 7 is my favorite. I like smoking weed with her and Mayuli on the balcony of Vapor 69, riding the high to another dimension and forgetting the spirit-breaking pleasures of living in underdevelopment.

We like to lie on that balcony and play with each other's toes, trailing pinky nails over our heels, soothing the calluses of this road with drugs and laughter. We like to infect each other. Mayuli claims to be male, but the three of us girls are on this pressure point in the map of Havana, pretending we're happy. Back when I was at ISA, I liked to find happiness in the most sensational ways with my friend E. Here, we're happy in the steadiness of our contemplation.

"My mother's doing better."

"So she's feeling better about his death?"

"His death gave her a reason to get busy again, you know how it is."

"Didn't she have a seizure on Friday?"

"Early Saturday morning. After we got the news that he died."

"What if the dead man possessed her, and her seizures are actually caused by the Commander's spirit?"

"No, chica. Though, maybe."

And we laugh and our toes laugh, rolling fits of laughter. Pamela once wrote a play about my mother's job. In it, a battalion of gray uniforms fight a giant *Aedes aegypti* mosquito whose stinger looks like a colossal phallus. As the battalion defends itself from the thrusting beast, it also defends the country from a slimy threat.

My mother was horrified by the idea, even though she was the hero of that piece of postdramatic theater. Pamela had portrayed her as a standard-bearer for the Federation of Cuban Women. My mother—no fan of the limelight—was unamused by the honor. She felt that the story was complicated and put her in a confusing spot. Mamá does not agree with ideological diversionism of any kind, especially in the arts and literature.

Mayuli never read the play because he was busy painting his room on Humboldt. As for me, the idea of that mosquito makes my skin tingle.

Pamela left her play unfinished, like my mother's life or the archeology of my Sunday or like that play *The Hard and Soft*, which my mother also disapproved of because it tackled another complicated subject.

Sometimes I dream about her heroic deed: I see her in her gigantic gray cape, flying recklessly around the gigantic mosquito. The play gives me a huge high, like the high from the fit of laughter we had just now. Mayuli, a snob with a dramatic streak, is radical, crazy; he's also the strongest one of us. Today he decided to put on a T-shirt with a photo of Fidel painted with red devil horns. As I stroke Mayuli's thigh, I picture my mother shredding his T-shirt with garden shears, my mother slicing into the shirt and Mayuli's chest. The Commander's face gets soaked in blood, and the cure is worse than the disease.

What's this laced with? Where'd you get this juice, this exotic morsel, this miracle herb? Mayuli got us some good stuff—Pamela and I are having fun. My head is a mosquito thrusting at the mourning weasels. My head's about to explode against Mayuli's thighs.

My mother should kill R. My mother should smash all the light bulbs in all the houses inhabited by the neighborhood weasels. You all need a mosquito to inject you with sperm and make you cry. You need to safeguard your country so your belly buttons will stop itching so much. You need an ice cream cone. You need herbal medicine.

This stuff is strong.

Mayuli rents out his room on Humboldt so people can get laid after leaving the gay bar, which is named after the same German naturalist. Pamela and I have a soft spot for the lovers that show up at that dive. Pamela and I are tingly and buzzed, and we make out like close friends. We gave it a shot once, but things didn't work out. Mayuli gets sentimental and starts talking about his grandmother, who died of pancreatic cancer. He says he can't live with the ache of that loss, that he never wants to paint again.

My mother should come and save the three of us, rouse us from this lethargy or exterminate us like just another plague infecting the country; she should pull us out of the drift. The purest thing my generation does: live adrift, lose ourselves in drift after drift, the poetics of drifts, adriftosophy, adrift in time, adrift in milk, insects incapable of love.

This is heavy. It's splitting my head in two. It's taking me out of myself.

No one wants to see a Fidel biopic, R. No one wants to see a film about his glorious olive-green life, even if it does resemble the life of a great actor—he was one of the talented ones. At the end of the day, if there's one thing that can be said about him it's this: He was a great actor.

The bed in that room on Humboldt is more pure than Fidel's bed, but then again, everyone harbors some resentment toward Fidel. Pamela puts on track 7 of *Elephant*

Family. Elephants and mosquitoes float in the sky. Afterward, we'll go to Humboldt to fuck a twink and let our phones get stolen and put *Elephant Family* on a USB for him, to distribute Pamela's music around what's left of the gay scene and mischief-making in Havana.

There's nothing left, I've spent all of it. Mamá won't be getting that thirty CUC. We go buy a little more grass and then sit on the Malecón to grieve and fling pure drama into the sea. Fidel will know these are morbid funeral rites, but he'll accept them anyway, because all good actors are clear on the fact that you have to graciously accept all tributes. I laugh until I forget about R's smell in my vagina. I laugh until my toes disappear and become a closed fist.

I hold the phone to my ear: me falling again and again to the floor. I listen to the recording over and over, enough times to erase R. Pamela and I sleep in each other's arms, sniffling.

My mother called me seven times. I hope she's feeling better and that she isn't disappointed. Pamela shows me photos from when she was a little boy. Nothing beats holding a trans woman on a Sunday night. She doesn't share those photos with just anyone, but we show each other everything: our STIs, herpes sores, zits, rashes, arteries hoarse from overexposure to being loved badly by Cuba, from loving badly. Pamela was born a boy, but who cares.

I wish I was deaf. Pamela wants me to be happy, but happiness only lasts as long as it takes me to polish off my ice cream, as long as the drugs, as long as the vague moment when R bribes me and then bruises a few of my bones, a moment whose sole purpose is to inspire him to finally write his biopic and pitch it to the national television company.

Mother-Heroine does not come. She was probably flattened by the Abate, by the fumigation chemicals. Mother-Heroine does not come for Pamela, or for me, so alone on the balcony, wondering if it's Monday already and if we'll ever find the phone that pansy stole from us at Humboldt two weeks ago.

Mayuli sets off to the bar in that T-shirt. Pamela and I fall asleep. What a pathetic weekend.

Pamela: your unforgettable voice and your throat. You're my only friend. The only thing she likes about Cuba is Tocopán, the Pan American Games mascot, though I guess she also likes Pepitos and his mischief. What I like about her is that she doesn't really know me. What I like about her is that we'll never really know each other. What I actually like about her is that we're attached at the hip, though deep down I know Pamela is too perfect and she'll get bored with awkward old me, because nothing I write or design is any good. Even though I know she's going to leave and that I'll have to stay, Pamela still saves me with her long silences and memorable speeches. Pamela and I understand the fate of friendships like ours, and we swore we'd be together after the cataclysm. We made a vow of love.

Pamela didn't want to come with me to the Muestra de Cine Joven party on Friday, so I had to go by myself. I think that's the reason I lost my earbuds and got this horrible bruise on my arm.

I don't have anything to do today. Ever since they "temporarily" closed the theater, I've been in a sort of limbo, which is how most people in Cuba live, a "temporary" limbo. The bruise. My right arm. Epilepsy. My sixteen-year-old sister. My arm. Limbo. Last Friday, a Friday like any other, me getting home. My mother on the floor. Monday. It's Tuesday. I don't know how I made it to Tuesday. Limbo.

Sometimes, another day passes us by, and Pamela and I don't even realize.

"And the money?"

"I spent it all."

"Aren't you going to eat?"

"I'm not hungry."

My sister is identical to my mother. She shares nearly all Mamá's obsessions: She hugs her when she gets home from work, prints the local CDR's political pamphlets about anti-mosquito campaigns, makes drawings for her to hang on her wall at work. We don't look anything alike, but the same blood flows through us.

My sister has a boyfriend. He's doing his mandatory military service. On Saturday, she went to her dad's house (we have different fathers—mine doesn't exist, hers is a good guy). Now she's walking around holding a glaringly stupid pink planner, writing poems even rosier than the covers, and putting frosted stickers of kisses on it for her boyfriend in confinement.

Despite being perfect, my sister causes my mother headaches: "You sound like your big sister when you say bad words, and I'd rather see you dead than lost like her."

I'm so bored I could die. There's nothing on TV—regular programs are on pause to give everyone space to mourn. I wonder what the kids are getting up to. The ones who have a computer or a console are probably alright, but the others will have to make do with schizo, over-the-top news shows (weasels find the clumsiest ways of giving tributes).

My mother won't turn off the TV or radio. When she's not down there commiserating with the weasels, she's trash-talking people on the weasel committee. When she's not lecturing me, she's rewashing my underwear because apparently it's not clean enough. They should be more commercially minded about the TV they produce, they should know that a eulogy is a work of theater meant to make you cry, that less is more, and nothing is too shiver-inducing—not the biography of a man or the pupils of people in the street.

"Could you turn it down?"

"Get to work."

"This country's fucked."

"Oh, will you be quiet already? All you're good for is screwing around. Go help your sister sort the rice and don't smoke in my house."

I won't fall off the wagon again. It was just one cigarette—I stole it right out of Mayuli's pocket. I've been craving a smoke since Friday, and the feeling won't go away.

"Fine, I'll help sort the rice, but then I'm going to Coppelia with Pamela for ice cream."

My sister is not like me. My sister makes a face when she hears Pamela's name. In our family, we all make the same face: we crinkle our brows, suck our teeth, look down on stuff we think is shit. To my sister, my friend and trans sister Pamela is a weird curiosity.

We usually slide right into Coppelia by saying we're going to Las Tres Gracias (the part for foreigners, where the prices are in CUC), and since we look like foreigners (thrifted clothes, uneven hair color, hairy armpits), the weasel attendants let us pass. Then we go straight up. The flavors are gross and always a surprise. Here, too, the news, and the news's insistence on seeming real.

Fidel's voice and the eye-watering billboards giving us our doctrinal vitamins. Pamela and I go all in and order four boats of chocolate ripple ice cream, since the other flavor is pineapple orange, and we refuse to let that anywhere near our mouths. In this place, this living museum, in a time as distant from my present as the Ten Years' War of 1868, there were once 101 flavors.

We used to work at the theater together. Pamela was the playwright and I was the costume designer, and we were both rising stars. But the theater "temporarily" closed after one of our plays, *The Hard and Soft*, was censored. I'd designed an outfit based on the work of my favorite artist, Tracey Emin—not her performances but her film and textile pieces. I made a black leather corset interwoven with needles and knives, because I've always identified with her body in *Why I Never Became a Dancer*. The story of her body is like mine. The little girl touched by all the men who wanted to touch her.

All the tables at Coppelia need to be fully seated, which means you're never alone. Today, Pamela and I are sharing a table with an old man and a woman with gold teeth who's sweating like she just got off the bus. The old man orders a twin scoop. I feel so bad for him that I give him five pesos to upgrade to a boat. The woman would do anything not to be next to the old man or to have to listen to me and Pamela making fun of everything. We look weird to her, with our tattoos and unevenly dyed blue hair. She also doesn't like that we smell of BO—very unpleasant.

The waitress brings our boats, and the woman says she wants a tub to go, pineapple orange. The woman, beautiful, Black, with perfectly almond-shaped eyes, is probably in her fifties, though she could pass for forty. The only thing I can't stand is the way she's looking at us. I mean, I guess she has the right to judge us back: We're a couple of stupid little white girls, and she's tired of having to put up with dumb shit from privileged white wannabe artists.

Suddenly, she isn't looking at us anymore—she's walking to the register with a neon yellow backpack. The waitress has left our boats on the table and is on her way to take care of the woman at the register, which is the kind of business she finds easier. The old man takes out a plastic bag and slips in the two mini-scoops from the twin scoop as well as the scoops from the boat. He gets up and leaves, and Pamela and I fail to notice that he doesn't pay.

We laugh, then start shouting. The waitress, alarmed, asks us to settle our check and keep our voices down—the country's in mourning. More laughter. The woman puts the tub of ice cream in her backpack. That's it for me, I won't need to eat anything else for the rest of the day. I can use the momentum to start a diet. The goal is to lose thirty kilos. Pamela is thin and sexy. . . Me, I'm the nice chubby designer. I want a new part to play.

I notice a bag on the floor, possibly left behind by the old man. I don't want to touch it, but then I get curious. Pamela gets sad.

"It's your fault the old man left his bag behind."

The woman says goodbye with a gold-toothed Cuban smile. I hope she doesn't take that ice cream on a bus, and I hope she doesn't forget us anytime soon.

At Pamela's house, we open the bag. Inside are two bread rolls, a notebook, and a pen. The notebook is filled with poems, short, unusual poems that make me want to cry. We read each other all the poems and then feel hungry again, but we're broke, and there's nothing in the fridge at Vapor 69. All we have is this balcony and the words the old man wrote to comfort us.

My phone dings. A text from the guy from the party: *Little Red Riding Hood, lemme at you. You got away from me on Friday.* I don't have enough credit on my phone to reply, and I also don't want to die in his Cuban alpha weasel-style Latin Americanist machismo. It's boring. I'd rather he bruised my arm and simply ceased to exist until the next party.

The woman is probably eating her ice cream or separating it into smaller containers to resell.

My mother and my sister must be having their rice. I prefer this hunger with Pamela, though I'm worried about the old man who lost his poems. Sure, the country lost it all—it lost the Ten Years' War, it lost what was hard and what was soft, it lost ninety-nine flavors of ice cream—but it gained us sitting on this balcony. We laugh like dying sopranos. Pamela and I will laugh at anything, at everything except these short poems that will be with us always. We read the poems aloud so as not to lose them. We find powdered milk, sprinkle in some sugar, and our intestines are relieved.

Before I go to sleep in my little room in Centro Habana, I take my sister's pink planner and copy the old man's poems into it. I hope she doesn't die of heartache for her boyfriend while he's doing his mandatory military service. I want to see her live and take care of my mother. I want them to never lose the sense of duty and belonging they have toward each other. My love for them has never been unconditional.

Mayuli got beat up yesterday, Pamela texts me. Mayuli isn't answering calls or texts. After Humboldt he went to get some rent money, or so Pamela says as I close my sister's planner and feel the sudden urge to lie down. Mayuli is in a fucked-up situation. It's not the same for us.

"I love your silhouette because it's music. You love nothing about me because I'm dead, and that's why I love."

Some of the old man's verses eviscerate me. I dream about the woman from Coppelia reselling her pineapple orange ice cream and wish her the best. If alcohol is banned this week of official mourning, then at least let there be cold, cold ice cream.

A chubby mulata woman made of pure joy once gave me a set of wax crayons from a top-notch brand—chrome colors that livened up my drawings. She gave them to me when I was in my first year at ISA.

That's how I met Yaneika, the curandera, the nurse, the sage. Two months ago, I got to know her a little better. I dreamed about her as well, her two big, plump hands that channel the whole world, the rivers and lands.

Our play had just been censored, and I was walking around with a fetus inside me. I had zero maternal instincts, just nightmares, nightmares where R took my child and made them go to sleep so he could erase everything that was lovely about them. Who really wants to give their child to Saturn to do with what he will? Who really wants to place all that innocence into guilty hands? Who really wants a shuttered theater, a child that isn't yours but is growing inside you? Who really wants to be a mother?

In addition to being a curandera, Yaneika is a nurse at Emergencias hospital. I asked her for menstrual regulation—no big deal. The fetus and I had come not a moment too soon. It was just a few days, a few cells. Yaneika eyed me with suspicion when she spotted me. She understood the look of desperation on my face, the childlike hurt, and she didn't say a word, or ask difficult questions, or judge me. Instead she planted a grandmotherly kiss on my forehead, placed her hands on my shoulders and the back of my neck, closed her eyes, and said: "You're tense, niña. Lost. You need to try and find some peace."

I noticed Yaneika was wearing mismatched earrings—a singular idea of the city, the island, the universe hanging from each ear—and extensions in her hair. I knew those blond ringlets had once belonged to some tormented soul in Havana who'd given up those dead cells for a good price. But these details didn't make her better or worse at practicing santería, better or worse at being a nurse, better or worse at knowing the world. What made Yaneika special was the tender spirituality of her approach and how she walked up to me without a word, like she knew the moment she touched me, like her hands understood my sadness better than any other hands ever could.

Yaneika took a clipper and passed it over my head, shaving off every trace of R. I needed to erase all those dead cells from my body one way or another. I gave her all my mistreated hair. I asked her to hold me. Not to tell my mother. I think my gut may have cleaved open like a wall collapsing deep in the desert. A big boom and a finale: bald, jobless, Yaneika's premonition, R's child in a pile of biohazardous waste at Emergencias hospital.

She asked me why I did it if it made me so sad.

"I'm dragging my half-dead body around like a dog with no future, no aspirations. I have nothing."

"That's one hell of a complicated way to put it, hija. Put your feet up, no hard work for you, nothing, niña, nothing, just rest, total rest. And talk to your mom. She understands what you're going through, she loves you so much."

"What my mother needs is for me not to exist."

R finding out and lashing me with a whip. R marrying me and bringing me to political actions and whispering State secrets in my ear. Yaneika sitting at the hairdresser picking the most unlikely hair possible to plant on her head, the blondest ringlets, which fall over her eyes, turning the real world inside Emergencias hospital into a lab room on an American TV show like *Grey's Anatomy*.

"Can I take something for the pain?"

"Ibuprofen, whatever painkiller you have at home."

"Will the pain stop?"

"Deep breaths and sleep, that's what you need."

I knew Yaneika, but the Yaneika I knew was different, no big thighs or truncated life. Yaneika had come to Havana on a train, like my mother, but she'd also been smarter than her and married an old man. After taking care of him, Yaneika got to keep his house. Meanwhile, Mamá got screwed over again and again.

"Don't say anything to my mother. She's half-dead like me."

"Be safe."

How was I supposed to tell R what he'd done? How was I, bald and tattered, supposed to tell him that I felt like a little tadpole? Maybe he'd have kids, but they would never be my kids. Who knows, maybe R used to have a big family that no one's met. I didn't know anything about R, so I had to use my imagination, make educated guesses.

In this week of solemn goodbyes, I think back to Yaneika's earrings (a golden sun and a glittering red drop). I think back to the trickle of blood, the metal tray. I think about how nothing else will ever be so painful. The world came to a standstill that afternoon, and before drifting off to sleep I saw pink stars and gruesome collisions of blood against my eyes, rushing to accuse me, rushing to say it'd be better if I didn't exist and stopped doing all the stuff that isn't supposed to be done with such nerve and such devastation.

Yaneika ran her hand over my head, with pity. I wonder what telenovela or show Yaneika is watching this week. It just so happens my period started today, and I feel shaky. The baldness was short-lived, just like the fetus, the mass, the baby weasel. All that's left is the phantom thrum in my gut. All that's left are Yaneika's hands on my neck, with all their heaviness and purity—when I don't feel like getting up but get up anyway, when I don't want to do or think the things I do, when I can't even imagine a different reality.

Yaneika and my mother holding hands in the most uncomfortable seat on the train. My mother and Yaneika hurting over Fidel's death. My mother and Yaneika sharing one glorious day as they traveled to the capital. Now they wave distantly to each other and share nothing, not visits to the hairdresser, not conversations about life. If Yaneika were to tell my mother I'd had an abortion, then my mother would go on about how I murdered a baby, and I'd have to explain to her that the reason abortion is legal in Cuba is that the Revolution understands this supposed drama is outdated, and that I hadn't felt anything. But that kind of response would upset my mother. My mother often gets upset.

"Mami, it's R's child."

"Don't be retarded."

"Mami, let me think."

"You try and think."

I look at the ceiling, sad poems and sad facts, and there, in love, sunk deep in my head, is the child, who I hear laughing; they must get sent to limbo, shorn hair and aborted children, they must end up in a limbo inaccessible to thought. I'd like to go back to my birthday, the birthday when I met Yaneika, when nothing had happened yet, that first year at ISA when Pamela and I met. My only consolation is going back to any place but this one. I wish I could take a train back along the same route my mother took to come to Havana. Maybe I'd find myself there.

Gray uniform: Here everything smells like urine and exhaust from the city's beat-up cars. The little campaigns have sought to be effective. Cold snaps are as effective against the plague as Abate chemicals. Mamá is in love with a meter reader. Meter readers don't wear uniforms, they wear fanny packs with meter readings and sunglasses. They don't believe in campaigns. If you give them a reasonable sum, the meter readers will tweak what the meter actually reads and lift the gray weight of electricity usage. It's called a counterattack plan. Mamá wears a gray uniform, while her boyfriend wears regular clothes in his line of work. Better to wear regular clothes, I think. Mamá loves her boyfriend.

My mother is drying out and so is my sister. This week of national mourning is officially a dry week. My father, wherever he is, is drier than I am—but who knows where he is, not even my aunt has any idea. My soul dries out. I'm dry, and I need to drink something, feel something, get up to something, dry-run into something.

Little Red Riding Hood, lemme at you...

I dial *99 and call him collect. "Got something to drink? I've got something for you."

I leave everything half-done and all there is inside me is a drought-etched fissure. These texts help me find the strength to get out of bed.

I don't know why, but I've always been a toxin-filled fissure. I have to rid myself of my toxicity. A body could change everything—his weasel body could change everything. He has a helpful way of smiling, and he's looking at me with lustful eyes. He reminds me of a woman I loved when I was nineteen. I'd like to pretend it was that woman who dug her fingers into my arm in the bathroom.

He refuses to acknowledge grabbing my arm and burning my hand with his cigarette at the Muestra de Cine Joven party. *You didn't have to brand me like that, babe, I was going to call you anyway, come over to your house anyway, act like I always do anyway—too breezy, too smiley, too easy.* Isn't that what all the weasels want?

The following facts are unimportant: When I meet a man for the first time I always know if we're going to sleep together one day, I really do. This is not me being cocky, but rather a truth about men and my know-it-all vagina.

Pamela doesn't like that I'm into him, Pamela doesn't like when I'm into anyone she didn't pick out herself. She doesn't get it. There's something about the crudeness and clumsiness of weasels that fascinates me—a kind of hetero masculinity that begs to be broken. And their sweat. And their animal stench that stands your hairs on end. I want to lie on their skin and get drunk because just thinking about my half-assed life, my dryness, disgusts me so much that I'll take anything. I laugh at the underground Siberia of weasels who won't drink for a week and still pretend they're feeling a once-in-a-lifetime happiness during a mourning ceremony for nothing.

What's happened to this country's men? Why do all men have such bad manners? Does this man think he's the Big Bad Wolf? Parnassian. Pragmatic. Phallocentric. "I don't wish to revel as I have reveled. I don't wish to suffer as I have suffered." Pamela has to understand that I'm self-destructive. Case in point: I thought it'd be a good idea to reply to his message with a phone call.

I like dialing *99. It's my signature and legal right to call people and have them pay—I should never be charged for calls, they should. I type in the make-them-pay code, *99. I dial his number hoping to turn into a corset interwoven with needles. I do it because I've got nothing better to do than write an apocryphal epistolary about censorship. Dry law for the weasels and remote-controlled children. He is the willing Wolf, while I am trying to be the "red" character from a fairy tale, the girl who lets the animal foot the bill for her phone call.

I want the dryness to reach my memory and for my memory to be blank and for the mourning drought to also dry out our expectations. And I'm thinking about my grandfather, who's been in my dreams every night this week. Along with all of my dead. I don't like Wednesdays, that's the reason, that's why I call him, so I can escape, because Wednesdays are when I think about my grandfather and my friend Alberto. Except that's a lie, I don't think about them—I don't even realize when I think about them.

Red because of the cape, not red like weasel blood. The weasels are red aficionados, easily dazzled by the bright-red splendor of the world. I have yet to be Little Red Riding Hood, I have yet to give consent, I have yet to feel regret and torture myself for all the Wednesdays when I don't think or feel: dry ditch, bone-dry, fissure for holding a weasel, empty fissure, totally empty, fissure to be filled with a dick.

"Come in, niña. Take your shoes off, I don't want you getting my floors dirty."

"It's not mud or anything, I'm just tracking in dirt from the street."

"Exactly."

"So silly."

Barefoot, I sit down on an ultramarine cushion. He breaks out some weed. This is no weasel. He puts on music, and it isn't what I was expecting, but it's fine. He's the biggest weasel of them all, truly, mortifyingly weaselly. You can smell it on him.

"What are you going to do with your life? Any idea? Do you make enough from theater to live?"

I want him right now. Big Bad Wolf, Big Wolf, Wolf: What I want is the bruise you left on my arm that hurts when I sleep on my side. The hole on that side of my chest. The blood that seeps from that hole, staining the floor, the blood drawn by the corset, blood that's watery, lukewarm, still lukewarm. I want a fissure filled with trash from a weasel who cares about his floor.

The journey begins with this bloodspill. He's not in mourning, he knows exactly why I'm here. One bowl and the smoke and it goes straight to my head and my fissure is drooling, my punctures, my logic, and my obliviousness and ambiguity are spitting me out too. While I'm on top of him, I'm thinking about my sister. It's not that I'm distracted. It's just that my brain can think and experience a thousand things at once. I have no idea if my sister's lost her virginity to her military service boyfriend, or any idea if she moves like me.

I rock back and forth. Hips require effective—rhythmically effective—coital mechanisms. I focus on my blood and on that hole, on how easily I gave myself to him, and I think about how I'm going to become just another option in his pirated porn collection, because something tells me he's filming us. This breaks my focus. The idea that this emptiness will be infinitely reproduced is the only thing that takes me out of the choreography. I rock back and forth, balancing on my decision to be the fairy-tale character who makes calls by dialing *99.

"Do you make enough from theater to live?"

"Theater is life."

"That's why I like you, bunny, because you're pure poetry."

"What a drag, don't be so corny."

"Little Red, life is misery."

"What's that one from? It's even cornier."

"That was just a bit of theater, Little Red, you're pure theater, that's right."

"This is a nice house. It's so quiet."

"Aren't you a designer?"

"Let's say I am."

"Design something for my house, something pretty, yes, big and delicious like you."

Pamela was right about this kind of guy—he thinks with his dick. I left everything half-done, my thoughts, my worries, my boredom. I left Wednesdays half-done and I left my eyes scanning the room for answers, the same exercise my sister and I do with the ceiling. The ceiling will tell us something. Through the figures emerging from the third-floor damp. A ridiculous sentence comes to me from the dead quiet of that little room in Centro Habana, the way my mother spins theories and comes to the conclusion: "My older daughter is a plague."

I'm a plague, I think to myself, staring at the ceiling while the Big Bad Wolf gives it to me good. The Big Bad Wolf's ceiling is dull—there's nothing up there to capture me.

I've become just another piece of unease, nothing to do, a state of futility and tedium in suspended purity. My own self-pity bores me, the stoppages, the rapid dilation of my vagina, anus, the rapid emptying, rapid disproportion between my mother's pain and the world's, between the familiarity of the old man who left behind his poems and my grandfather, between Sunday's weasel and this one who's sliding into me on top of a dining table. Eyes trained on the ceiling.

A generation lost to contemplating nothing but the ceiling. Here with him, I don't want to finish anything, say anything true, feel anything; I fled the dryness and came here to tend to it, to feed it this vague moment of forgettable penetration, this bad, melodramatic conversation that doesn't contain even a hint of fairy tale or truth.

I want to drop by Pamela's house and tell her this guy is a terrible lover, he doesn't even breathe on your neck, he's too focused on his dick and thinks that by grabbing my hair he can teach me something about love.

In my backpack, there are a couple stills of Leningrad and a bottle of vodka. My stomach hurts. I'm a thief, a bum, the dregs of a dry Wednesday and all the Wednesdays that aren't officially dry.

Leningrad: The meter reader thinks the USSR still exists. Mamá thinks the Revolution still exists. My vagina thinks love still exists, that this is love, to be a spectral woman who lets herself be drawn along by inertia. My sister thinks I was good before I lost myself. When my sister saw me come in with my bald head, she started crying. My mother says I traumatized my sister. Maybe her tears are the closest thing to something that existed before I was born. The meter reader from the USSR thinks electricity still exists. My vagina thinks love is what the old man at Coppelia described in his poems and that the best thing anyone can do is let someone stick it in and make all that darkness more bearable. Which is wrong, I know, except maybe it's not.

I want to see my ex-boyfriend, the theater manager, the philosopher. I miss him. The thing I miss most is his smug pessimism, which makes him detest and judge everything.

He and I came up with the idea of weasels: pleasureless creatures who've been domesticated and live hypocritically, tolerating the heteropatriarchal mechanisms of power because it suits them. To define a weasel is to define how I am different from everyone else, the childlike arrogance that makes me think it's possible to distinguish me from myself.

I never told my philosopher about R. He doesn't know that R's teeth are stained black. The gallant gentleman of my thirty-CUC Sundays has the most disgusting gums in the world, and his teeth are like a great big oil slick. I guess there could be some desire lurking under my repulsion.

Sometimes I dream that R is pulling my hair, that the only thing I want is for him to pull my hair. That's why I gave my hair to Yaneika—so this torture being used to destroy me wouldn't lead to a new archaeology of knowing (it's like R became my new philosopher-boyfriend), one that conceives of Cubanness in hunger, in entomology, in prostitution, in the Cuban police, in the history of the Centennial Generation, in *Lunes de Revolución*, in acts of repudiation, one that conceives of Cubanness in things me and my boyfriend the philosopher have never experienced. Now there wasn't anything to pull or anything to regret.

Screaming things in my ear. Raping a dead woman.

Raping me like my head was inside an oven. Raping me like he was going to bust my teeth on a concrete counter. R justifies rape with the concept of a prostitute's consent, only I don't know when I said yes or when I decided I wanted it to stop, but I live by that consent (I have no idea what makes me any different from the male whores who go to Humboldt and who Pamela and I talk about like they're bad stage actors. I should learn from them to be less horrifying).

R has revolutionary attributes. In addition to majoring in military strategy, he studied philosophy, and he's forgotten how to be an ordinary man. He doesn't feel like a common man, but he knows he is a weasel. R insists on smiling, but he doesn't know. His stained teeth remind me of my mother bleeding from her mouth. The repulsive part of me that relishes the tongue in that mouth on Sundays is also what's left of the revolution in my body.

My mother despises alcohol because it reminds her of my father. It's possible I made this up, but that's my theory, that my mother hates drinkers because they remind her of my father. Except my father has nothing to do with the feeling

I sometimes get that I've been dragged along the floor, pulled by the ears or the tongue, had my skin lifted off.

There are two very different philosophers in my life, two philosophers who have experimented on me. . .

My mother is a hardworking woman who fights mosquitoes. It's a social fight she wages every day, but then she convulses on the floor and bleeds from her mouth. It really is ridiculous of her to claim that she doesn't know what R does to me, what we do on Sundays. That's my mother: a common woman who isn't interested in being the heroine, who doesn't even really believe that *Aedes aegypti* should be eradicated. My mother has hushed the love story between me and R. She's seen me go to all our appointments. In her head, she must think I'm helping R with a novel, a million-page list of commandments about Cuba's political system, as if I could use my vision to help anyone write a never-before-written treatise about Cuba's Cubanness.

R obviously doesn't need my help with his writing. The only thing he needs is to educate the lost youths proliferating in his country with their abhorrent logic: "Mamá, with or without hair, with or without your permission, R needs me, he needs to stick it in me while I lie there like a dead woman."

Now I'm remembering the first time I masturbated. I must've been ten or eleven. I took my pillow, put it between my legs, and jerked it against myself over and over, rubbing it against my adolescent clitoris. There was nothing wrong with pressing the pillow against my body and knowing it wasn't enough, but it was enough to know I could spend another hundred hours there, feeling the pillow the way you feel a surge that isn't there but somehow still delivers a galactic dimension to your vulva. At ten, with a pillow between my thighs, I discovered another realm.

I have a few ideas for a play. Maybe they'll reopen the theater. But not right now, they say, nothing at all for now. They have repairs to do, contracts to renegotiate, everything's going to be transformed, they don't need a corset to know that a parasite was gnawing at the bowels of the National Theater. Maybe they'll reopen it the week after next or next month. I know we'll put something else on, anything else, but not *The Hard and Soft*—that, we can't even talk about anymore.

I don't want to spend my life doing nothing. I want to have a salary like a weasel, like any regular person. Right now I'm in limbo, up in the air, right now I'm walking in lots of directions that look the same but aren't.

My philosopher, the theater manager, says: "Let's discuss Foucault, it's such a turn-on."

He pushes my legs open on top of his desk and tears off my panties, which were really pretty and had lasted several years. They recommend changing out your underwear every three months—in Cuba, this doesn't apply. He turns me onto my back and doesn't worry about being careful, he's never been careful, and my skin has only gotten tougher (like female weasels, who after their first rape end up sharing food with the male weasel). He breaks me and everything stings.

It's such a turn-on to think about Foucault alongside that ache. I think about Tracey Emin dancing. He opens and closes me like a glass jar that falls to the floor and shatters, then gets scooped up and put back together only to fall again; I keep falling and coming apart and reconstructing myself in a work of recursive theater. These thoughts don't paralyze me. I feel lighter if I think about art while these men pump away, or if I think about images like a broken plate or else think about my mother and jelly, I feel lighter if I disconnect from this scene, if I obediently break myself, if I fake my pleasure, if I imagine myself going home with no underwear on, thighs burning in the humidity.

My mind is always everywhere at once except when I'm about to come, which is when my head feels clearest. Since the age of ten, I've found it easy to distance myself from the world when I'm about to orgasm with my pillow, my right hand. My head is inside me, there it is, the ceiling opens.

"Let's talk about Foucault, not hunger. Hunger is such a turnoff."

"I have a secret."

"You don't have any secrets. But if you do, I don't want to hear them."

"But I want to tell you."

I really ought to have a secret, I think to myself, and not a girly secret. If my mother has a seizure, I put Abate in her mouth, use Abate to kill the effects of the bleeding tongue and the indents left by her teeth when they bite down, I watch her die from the poison of her own battles and think about that tragic moment, thoughts coursing through my head like something irredeemably simple, fateful.

He applies Abate between my legs. Maybe this will teach me not to think of myself as a nymphomaniac and to adjust to the mud and unease on the streets and to the dry law for the proletariat on this week of national mourning. Today is Thursday. Limbo. Captivity. Limbo. Every Thursday, eating, Abate.

I didn't actually come to talk about technologies of the self, and I didn't call him up because I'm interested in his silence. My philosopher hasn't texted me in two months. He's fallen for a 6'5" actress who doesn't love him. I came to share the bottle of vodka I took from the Big Bad Wolf's house a couple hours ago, to smoke, to perform the banal exercise in submission that helps him slowly rid himself of the rotten things inside him. He wants to give it to me hard, philosophically speaking: hardness exorcizes the male weasel.

What this means is making my clitoris spin and whetting his tongue on the metal surface of the corset draped over my back. Telling him a secret precisely because he doesn't want to hear it. Thinking about R, thinking about him constantly and feeling ashamed. I didn't come here for any particular reason, I didn't even miss him that much.

Walking. Running. Buying. Swallowing. Talking. Feet covering ground in the city. Biting. Sunken thorax. Music turned off. Everything quiet. Everything gloomy and boring and sad. A bunch of people trying to die and laugh and be happy. Peeing. Pooping. Cleaning. Everything's been different since Friday, but my reality is immutable, therefore it's everything else that has changed. My thighs are caked with mud, my vagina is drinking, what a stroke of luck that everything's changed. Everything changes again and again. Even thighs that chafe against each other change, burn after burn, coitus after coitus, lover after lover, weasel after weasel.

The "specialists" came to the theater and shut its doors, forgetting that a theater's doors should always be open. The specialists are a kind of refined weasel, the kind whose dumb little powers make them grand. My philosopher and I despise the specialists. This philosopher doesn't matter in my life, he really doesn't, but he was my boyfriend and at the theater he managed things like hammers, nails, paint, curtains, makeup, and contracts for lighting and sound technicians. What does matter is the pillow, the liftoff, the body dragged across the floor because it's convulsing.

He carefully applies the Abate, then penetrates me phallically, calculating exactly when his dick's metaphysical effect should hit, his milk, his limp dick and its old-fashioned milk, his hard dick and its alienation from communism, capitalism, and the thousands of counters where I let his dick change the world, change the world of every Cuban in the world, change the great theater of Cuba in the world after the death of the Revolution's historic leader.

Moments like this, I think to myself that it'd be better if I could swallow a drug that sends me to sleep and puts me on pause, something truly immutable that takes my mind back to when I was eleven years old and there was no drought, or burning, or limbo, or weasels circling me like they circled Alberto, so they could hit me again and again. Now I feel like throwing up, and everything is spinning or opening and closing or wavering like a trapeze. I don't even know what it is I took. Outside this meeting, I am confronted with a life without theater, which is like a life without living, like the life of my mother and all the regular people who let themselves be broken.

I leave my philosopher's house and head to R's. It's Thursday, but I want to do myself damage. I can take it. R will let me in if I come to him toughened up by the other weasel. He'll be happy if I come to him drunk. My tendencies, which run counter to revolutionary morals, excite him.

4:00 PM – January 18, 2020
Café Le Relais de Belleville

Dear Mary,

I just ordered a double espresso, it's the only way to get real coffee in this country. Today I said no to him, I said no because I can't stand him, he's a ridiculous old man, he thinks I belong to him, an object without desires, like some sort of slave. I don't know if I told you, but at the office there's this vegan antiracist feminist who knows us, she says she met us in Havana. Well, the world is full of people who know each other and don't realize, through degrees of separation, we've met James Franco and Lady Gaga, remember the producer who showed us photos of herself with them? In some ways it's like we've met them. The only person I actually wish I'd met is Kurt Cobain. One time we crashed a film party here, the première of a François Ozon movie, Gérard got us invitations. She was so beautiful, of course, Marine Vacth. Gérard tells everyone I'm a famous playwright that he got out of Cuba because State Security was going to throw me in jail for *The Hard and Soft*. He makes up stories and makes me repeat them like they're true, sometimes he looks at me with pity, sometimes he looks at me with desire, I think he sees me as his pet or his property, I'm like an expensive Armani suit he's just bought, that's what he thinks of me, I'm a piece of fabric tailored with glee, with a label and a price tag. Anyway, the woman from work says she remembers us from a film festival, she said she assumed we were girlfriends, I told her we're sisters, I didn't want to say anything, but that's what came out. Then I went home, took off my shoes, took off my coat, poured myself a glass of wine, and wondered if we were sisters, milk sisters, life sisters, blood sisters, so many moronic thoughts ran through my head as I worked through that bottle of wine, one thought pulling in the next, and I remembered how you made me feel less alone and how you made me feel more beautiful, we were good for each other. Last night I went to bed late, alone, unshowered. Today I took a long hot shower, it's been a long time since I showered. I've gotten used to not showering, I don't know, it's like every shower takes away my desire for something, like the water strips a piece of memory from my skin. I went to the Gustave Moreau museum for the third time this year. I thought of you as a sister there too. At the museum exit I met up with a lover. Gérard can't know, but I like to go cruising, and I ask them to call me by the name my father gave me, sometimes I tell them my name is Pamela and sometimes I give them your name. I'm sentimental, and I hate work, I hate getting to work and having people ask me the same questions and smell my perfume and say, after all these years, have you tried this? At the party I made a fuss the way I like to, someone decided to talk about how Xavier Dolan was an idiot and I had to defend him like he was Cuban. I don't like it when jealous Parisians talk about him like that. I have no idea what films you're watching, we were always watching the same old movies. The coffee's gone cold. Take care. Hugs to your mother and sister.

The Respectful Whore

A dramatic poem by Mary Guerrero
(Jean-Paul Sartre, one of the century's most lucid minds, visits Cuba.)

I'm sure you already know what became of me as a whore and a vagrant, what became of me as a symbol in a symbolic country that only engages with theater that is symbolic. My symbolic fate as a whore and a vagrant in a red diary penned by men.

With their drooling jawbones they sweat and suture symbolic fictions about my teeth and my breasts. They laid hands on me and said I was not the misunderstood woman I claimed to be. They said I was a diabolo in the hands of a little girl. They said I was a ball to be batted with a rifle. Let's slug her till the red of her lips stops arousing us so much. They said whores know nothing about politics, that whores know nothing about plans to invade the Bay of Pigs, they said whores don't know their way around politics because the furthest thing from politics is prostitution.

As for me, I wanted to be a famous actress, and I could've been one too, but you don't want my life story, you want me to tell you about Miriam Acevedo, or to mention some famous actress who claims to have been me and thinks that all it takes to be me is to live my life, to slap on a cute smile for the photoshoot: "Move like this, whore. Touch yourself like this, whore. Whore, your eyes, your dark eyes, your charcoal eyes of a whore who never learned to feel this way, close your eyes and imagine that I'm your prince, picture me inside you. You're a gate-crasher, whore, you're a gate-crasher in a skirt. Let's pluck out those chrysalis tears. Quiet, whore."

You want to know what my history might have to say about this place, what fluidity and emptiness may explain about this place. Fleshiness and juicy tears don't want to refer to this place because this symbolic place doesn't exist. What does exist is me, on this stage, but the place, the dimensions you seem to perceive here, they do not.

Film? My favorite film? What do I wish my legs looked like? The first time I went to the movies? The movies? Have I told you about the first time I was paid for sex? Have I already told you why I took that train? Why I don't dream of being a mother? My breasts? Good sex? Why I dream about my son, my dead son? My recurring dreams every night? About snakes? The snakes . . . I've seen serpents and I've seen screwed-up expressions and I've seen flesh and I've seen limp dicks and I've felt the full-blown reality of those movies in my guts, playing at happy endings with my proboscis, sucking and sucking my own legs. I can love anyone, I can mold myself in such a way that I relish in skin, in padlocks, I can savor the sleep in someone's eyes and blanch with the salt of tears on a belly. I want it, I want a tentacular embrace, hands on me, they say, rub your eyes. I can love anyone because beauty isn't strange, and I'm not indifferent to beauty that fades away layer by layer.

The president came to see *Happy Birthday, Mr. President*. He said to me in a low voice: "Oh, the truth in this play! Theater is wonderful. I can feel Lizzie's anguish all the way from here behind these glasses."

I never tired of my fate as a historic figure in Cuban theater, or wringing every drop of juice out of the batiste curtain, so hard and so soft. I do get tired of your eyes and your clumsy hands groping my hips, dicing up my flesh, grinding my hide until you can extract little hollows to sell to the highest foreign bidder as the priceless idea of feminine Caribbean pleasure.

Replace pleasure with the sacrifice of pleasure. Replace sex with the sacrifice of sex. Replace meaning with a disciplined society of people who don't know me, who don't know my little holes and the memory of my little holes. Replace love with the unattainable love of my ass atop the National Theater.

Riddled with all these perforations, I walk over here, I walk over the muck, I walk over your muck, I walk over your bones and your torso, I walk while tracing my clitoris with your limp dick. I feel nothing, now I really feel nothing, and suddenly the only thing I'm suffering from is the stiffness of your love. In the stiffness, the silliness, of your little bell. In the silliness, the stiffness, of your little program. I feel nothing. Not even getting railed makes me feel something. Not even tearing myself into vouchers makes me feel something. Not even ossified monsters make me feel something.

I'm so grateful for all the outrage, all the love, all the beautiful women stepping on my spirit, kissing my spirit, rubbing themselves on a character to make something resembling the sensuality of a whore who hides a Black man, who saves a Black man, and that's the perfect ideal for a savage ideology where almighty good fights almighty evil. Where in a good and evil place does a whore lay her eyes?

When I first came to this place, the energy was different, people enjoyed other things, and I felt welcome. Later it became beautiful, sensational, I have clear memories of success, of the approving din:

"The whore is here. The whore is ours. The whore is the national whore. The respectful whore is the most whorish whore of all the whores with the right to be Cuban. Long live the whore. May she open her mouth, may she weep, may she kiss, may she reclaim a place for women, may our whoreforsaken history not be constrained to a whore's butt swelling after it is caned by the seminal whore who says, I open and swallow, I suck and swallow. The whore says she's getting banged up on this stage set that is a prison. The whore bangs up mimetic representational theater with a handkerchief, a là Simone. The whore says she knows love is in danger, that the revolution is in danger, that pleasure is in danger, and man is always made to make up his mind."

Sartre got there and sat down and said, I've ushered in another chapter of history, baby, I was told I'd be taken care of, have my ass wiped, my nipples sucked, be told, I've drunk the future of this island from you and it seems healthy to me, and clean, let's take a picture and say, Give me some cow's milk, baby, give me a federated future, baby, give me a corner where I can park my ass and we can give each other tongue, lick out the sweetness with nothing but our tongues and our countercultural desire, you can split in two like a beat and pick a yam up off the floor and scrape off the red earth with your toenails, suck off a whole theater, the audience in the theater who say:

"I don't eat dick. I don't eat shit. I don't eat fear. I don't eat squash. So put your cherry in the audience's corneas and say, I'm so weak, Sartre, I'm so weak, I'm so weak because I can't feed my kid, I've got nothing, I'm so weak, because I walked around naked onstage in *La Celestina*, I'm so weak because I met Fidel at a party and I asked him to take me away, wrap your arms around me, Fidel, I wanted to be Charlotte Corday, but I let my breasts get flattened.

"The actors are moving slowly, Sartre, but I'm not acting, I write in my diary: I'M A WHORE. I'M A WHORE. I DON'T EAT DICK."

What do I think about that pig Fred? What do I think about that pig Kennedy? What do I think about that pig Fidel? What do I think about that pig Sartre? The one I hate most of all is the senator. I slept with this Black man, if only he'd held me for a bit longer, if only I'd pressed myself against him, the only tender thing I've seen here is this Black man's eyes, the only thing here that hasn't felt ruthless is this Black man's eyes, the only pure thing is the Black man's future in my eyes.

I think about his children, a whole gaggle of children to feed and teach to dream. Would you know how to love a child with the same electric love you have for every little piece of your life, for every scrap of your flesh that you carry in your mouth?

We open our mouths and receive the seed of the men who make revolution, the men who say, Open your mouth, change that gesture, open your eyes, change your hair, change your body, change your voice, change your contortions, swarm in the air and scream, Long live, long live this Revolution, may the wind lift your dress, may you be drizzled with semen and like it, because you're a whore and whores can't make revolution.

When I close my eyes, when even all the way from over here I knock back this drink, I dream of Marilyn. I dream of my snakes and my snakes dream of an answer for you.

The snakes are closing in on me, they weave between my legs and then leave me here, it's always the same with them. Streets, corners, ramps up, ramps down, intersection of Infanta and Carlos III, Reina, dirty alleyways, blood, vomit, rape, drugs, alcohol, a police officer finds the corpse and says, But this isn't Marilyn, this is inconceivable, but this one isn't respectful, this one's to blame for the state of the world, because this one isn't a woman, this one's a man dressed as a woman, look at her, we can't show the mess of the shoulders, the gaping along the ribs, we can't show this body on the news.

Once you're a character you don't get to choose where you want to be, time decides for you and for the men, the directors, the presidents, the playwrights, the dictators, the professors, the academics, the writers, they say: "She's just a big whore."

You are the rest, the dregs of a thought, the emptiness of a misrepresentation, you're this shift's goods, the patriarchal harbor of concentration camps and jokes cracked in Ukraine about the eyes of women who were born as empowered socialists. And when they open my mouth for me, it's not me, I'm not the one speaking when they say a name, my name, and I wrap my arms around this Black body that I am going to protect.

I wish I could say I was alive.

I'm not a prodigal daughter. That's why I stayed here, I couldn't go back, I wouldn't have been welcome, no matter how many doses I took, I couldn't go back. I can tell you about my sister—we are all sisters. He laughed at her, spat on her, did not let me cry or breathe, laughed over me, mocked us, repeated that revolutionary gesture, we're going to split her in two until she dies like the whore she is.

I took the gun I saw in his pocket, I took the gun I saw in the pocket of the pants he'd tossed on the floor. I put a bullet in his head. My dead sister, eyes white. The other men pounded on the door because they heard the gunshot and wanted to kill me. I jumped out the window and got on the first train.

My sister among the snakes spitting barbiturates, my sister justifies the means so that *Lunes de Revolución* can say: This is our whore, and she is the whore who stands against capitalism.

My sister among the snakes offers affordable blow jobs on Malecón and 23, my sister justifies the means and helps extralegal sex trafficking proliferate like an illusion of sexual freedom and proletarian solidarity.

My sister is the National Theater, and she has a tongue that can freely fornicate atop a tablet that reads: YOU ARE THE REST.

My sister is wearing a mask and wants to write poems to justify the tepidness of her being in this atemporal spasm of acritical socialism she was raised in: "You are the rest."

Women, whores, the rest, get quiet, repeat, blind, they say, here is the Black man, the accused, here is the author's act of indulgence as they take a seat in the National Theater and run their hand over my dyed-blond head, over the warmth I've felt here when I mention my name and weep like a serpent chopped to pieces in a place called Puriales de Caujerí, which no one knows except my sister and me, the authors of this diary.

"Lizzie has just moved from New York to the American South. She is in her apartment with a man. The Black man knocks. He has been charged with a crime. Lizzie was on the train. Lizzie is his only witness.

"The Black man makes her promise to tell the judge the truth if she is called to testify. Though Lizzie doesn't want any trouble, she swears to tell the truth. The Black man leaves."

4:00 PM – February 18, 2026
Café Le Relais de Belleville

Dear Mary,

    My boyfriend and I have been in therapy for a few weeks now, that's why I haven't come to the café to talk to you. We're going to try to adopt. I want to be a mother, but I don't know if I'm ready. I wonder if you're a mother now, I can't picture it, it's kind of hard for me to picture you. He moved in with me recently. The apartment belongs to Gérard, but I can stay as long as I want, it's all the same to him if I spend the rest of eternity here with another man. My boyfriend is a lot younger than me, but he has money, anyone in this place can be the heir to a vineyard. I haven't met his family yet, he says they're not ready. For the second time in my life, I'm a rare bird to my boyfriend's French family. It doesn't matter. He's really fragile, which is the total opposite of Gérard, and he's been lonely all these years, we understand each other, I met him just out of rehab, but

I told you that already, it's just now I think that, in some ways, all we've done is take care of each other, and that's why we need a kid, to put that care on someone else, it's getting to be too much for just the two of us. He complains to our therapist about my silence, he says I'm really quiet, and the therapist tells him it's out of nostalgia or fear or maybe because I'm an immigrant or because I'm trans. The therapist says I need counseling, no doubt in my country I didn't get the right kind of counseling. I sit there silently, and remember how I used to be so strong and talkative, the impression I have is that I never shut up, but now I'm quiet, I only say the bare minimum, and I don't get into arguments over stupid shit like everyone else here. I'm not interested in talking about cheese or wine, I'm not interested in talking about Cuba or what's become of the country, I'm not interested in anything except him, his desires. We just hired an interior decorator for the baby's room, we don't know where we're going to get the baby from but we already have a list of names. I even thought about your name, but I haven't said it out loud because he's not going to like it. I think my silence probably has to do with not being comfortable speaking French, maybe it has to do with the language itself, maybe some languages are for speaking and others are for staying quiet, because you just know you'll never be able to say anything honest in them. Sometimes it happens that after speaking French all these years, I still get corrected by people who claim they don't understand me. Who say: What you said doesn't make any sense. I just pictured you and your mother living in my apartment. I feel a little lonely, the only thing I want is for him to touch me, for him to be inside me, to tell me: You're the mother of my child. It's the only thing that makes me feel good, can you believe it, it's like I spent all those years waiting to come to Paris to satisfy a boy who wants to be a father just so he can have someone else to take care of. Meanwhile, all I want is to take care of him, for him not to have nightmares, for him to love me, picture me naked, kiss me all over, and rub saliva into my eyes to help me see better. I guess this is what love is, this thing I feel for him, like the love I felt for you. I told you one time that I wasn't sure about the love we had for each other, I said that, but I was wrong, now I'm sure it's the only real thing I've felt in my entire life.

STATION

We have very few valuables. My mother didn't inherit anything particularly good from her family. My mother hadn't deserved the vintage dinner service, she hadn't deserved any valuable memories that could be touched, exchanged, or delivered to an antiques dealer with a knack for theft. This country is like my mother. The city is filthy, and the weasels pretend they're doing just fine without booze. I don't see what's so heroic about abstaining. As far as I'm concerned, it's the addicts who are the heroes, because they know themselves, they can sniff each other out.

This is Fidel's legacy: addiction. Power is the most addictive substance ever invented, and family heirlooms are an important marker of absolute power. I can't bring myself to love a hero who demands signatures and agreements, who imposes and indoctrinates. It's Thursday, not Sunday for the Defense, and ever since high school I've cultivated a careful disinterest in all collective decision-making. I am foreign to the weasel movement, to crowds, to the designs of a dizzying people.

I move by myself. My mother and sister move in step with the other weasels. It's the path of least resistance. But I like to stay isolated.

R has so many valuables in his family history, it's immoral. I'm not talking about books or about copyist paintings—I'm talking about collectables.

Fidel, naked, with his hairy chest and muffled voice and shaky hand. R and Fidel sitting together at the last supper. Now he is dust on the asphalt, and thousands of people march over his legacy. This is what I'm thinking about, about people trampling his legacy because it truly doesn't matter, nothing matters, and trampling things is the path of least resistance. My family's legacy is a photo album. We won't make a lot of money off of it. We accept this and move on.

I haven't heard any updates on Mayuli, though word is they didn't hit him, but they did take him into custody. Probably because his little room on Humboldt tarnished their image of the Revolution. Humboldt, where he threw countless parties despite the country being in mourning, where he let men traffic in sex as a form of socialist struggle: weasels on weasels, machos on machos, foreigners on weasels, machos on foreigners. The party at Humboldt was out of control.

The Cuban way of life doesn't come with sexually disturbing relics, it comes with a hero idolized by weasels. There's no trafficking in flesh—there is nothing. Here, there are busts. That's why men are so evasive in their love, because their romantic ideal is a woman who's asleep, passed out, unconscious, a woman who won't remember. That woman is Cuba: marble, motionless, she lets herself be trampled by crowds of weasels. She drinks the tea.

The weasels, R and Fidel, have the same opinion of me. They think I'm weak. They think that if they stick it in me, they'll grow. Up until now, I haven't been even a little bit countersexual, and my logic reproduces the logic of money and my mother's logic with the meter reader: I let a sense of obligation be imposed on me too. I read things stupidly, as if I were reading the electricity meter.

The first time R walked into our little room, my mother smiled at him from the hallway as my sister gabbed with some friend of hers on the phone about the K-dramas they were watching. I was in the living room reading the diaries of Katherine Mansfield, thinking I'd write a play with Pamela. My mother swung open the door and laughed. This is how she introduced the weasel to her artist daughter. She sat him down at the table, made a point of offering him the right chair—the one that doesn't need to be glued back together—then stared me dead in the eye in a clear sign of complicity and sold me with more skill than an African mother hoping to strike a marital agreement for her daughter. R thought I should be more feminine, that I had a disheveled hippy look.

"She has a degree in set design, but she's written poetry for as long as I can remember. She's very smart and hardworking."

R looked at my book and came out with some sexist bullshit. I whispered to myself: "Guaiacol tablets, balimanate of zinc." I don't know why, but saying these words seemed to shield me from him. R should've been marching in the procession, he should've been giving interviews, he should've been sad and scared shitless at the sight of Fidel's body. But R is a hypocrite.

He fixed me with his gaze, and since I didn't answer his questions, turning instead to his manuscripts on the table (the only sweetness came from those manuscripts, which smelled of typewriter), I figured something in me must've filled him with confidence; that, in a way, we shared a whiff of rot, of old type.

Faithful as ever to her principles of misery and blindness, my mother offered me to him like a recipe. She gave me a little push, told me to visit him on Sunday to help with his books, his scripts, his novels, and advised me to give up theater, which is a world full of birds and sick people and whores. She preferred to set me up with a retired military officer who had a two-story house of his own, a house where the weasel wrote fiction for presses I'd never heard of, ones Fidel would be proud of. Right there—that's where she preferred to see me.

That's how a bilateral agreement was struck between my hippy designer's world and R's world. I didn't raise my hand or cast a vote, I just thought about Mansfield drinking goat milk to cope with the loneliness. I imagined Tracey spinning and spinning, then I stuck needles in my hands and thought: "How hard can it be to read some sad old coot's manuscripts?" Back then I had essays and words. Now I have this sinking feeling, the feeling that I've inherited nothing from my family and those manuscripts are laughing in my face because they think I'm painfully vulgar. They don't like the musty smell of my used vagina. This Thursday our meeting was like a goodbye.

R usually swirls his whiskey with his fingers. Sometimes he acts like there's some sort of understanding between us: "When I was your age, I was always busy."

"Hmm, I can't picture you at any age except the one you are now."

"What is it you want?"

"I want to change this moment."

"What do you want to change?"

"I don't know. Myself."

The next Sunday I went back to his house. I had no idea what to expect; I had no idea that sometimes the sun, the tobacco, and the manuscript were all there waiting to laugh at me. The objects—the family heirlooms, vanity kits, and the hoariest kinds of memory—all pretended not to see my irreverence. Maybe I should've followed the herd, maybe I *was* following it. The only things that I can actually remember are the objects and the manuscript. The rest is this circular movement, limbo, a failed ideal, the beginning and end of every Sunday.

On Thursday, R doesn't talk to me about anything.

On Sunday, R will talk to me about a novel he's writing about the Angolan war (he said he was going to drop everything for the novel; the biopic would take time). He will serve me a cup of tea. He will look at me sadly, unsmiling, and not leave any bite marks. His house has the most valuables I've ever seen in one place. That won't make me miserable—it will fill me with joy, the joy of a poverty so vast it can't be measured. I hope the day never comes when my mother will have to be guilty of everything—but it isn't Sunday yet, this hasn't happened.

I stumble home, another sad Thursday, the TV programming laughing in all our faces.

My sister comes up to me. I can see in her face that she doesn't have any smiling left in her, and the little bags under her eyes tell me she's been crying.

"Tata, come sleep with me. The poems were so lovely. Did you write them?"

"I stole them from some old guy."

"Sleep next to me, I'm sad."

"Did something happen between you and your boyfriend?"

"Go on, come sleep with me."

Humboldt: a bar for fags and rent boys. A hole in the wall. Mayuli's apartment is on the next block, so it's ideally situated as a place to host cultural exchanges. Or was, because Mayuli isn't coming back. We don't know much except that it's bad. I love how decadent this bar is. I love what Alexander von Humboldt has written about this island. In *Political Essay on the Island of Cuba*, he talks about mud and slavery, he talks about me and my decadent friends who let themselves be penetrated and call themselves pansies in order to paint the Cuban night with something more than just darkness. This week the doors stay closed. We walk in and sit onstage. We walk in and sing karaoke. We make out with twenty fighter types, latch onto the promising young specimens of Cuban fauna. Humboldt's flora spits in our ears. I've lost earrings and piercings in Humboldt, I've lost my inhibitions among all those twinks, travestis, pansies, fags, locas, sluts: *Political Ecology on the Island of Cuba*. Shame I couldn't go this week. Shame that Mayuli and R don't know each other, secondary flora and fauna.

It's already Friday, another day. Pamela calls to tell me Gérard, her new French lover, wants to take us out to lunch to discuss an art project. My mother puts on her uniform and leaves. My sister puts on her school uniform to go to a tribute. I feel like I'm going to explode. There's so much inattention and innocence behind this uniformity that, charm aside, I feel completely detached from what the uniforms say: We've mass-produced a way of life and then pushed it onto you.

Gérard asks how we're feeling about the fateful event: our first laugh of the afternoon. Nothing really matters to us—we spend most of our time striking a pseudointellectual pose that makes us feel good, like drugs.

Gérard was the first to hear the news, he says. While I was bopping around the party for the Muestra de Cine Joven, he was leaving Fábrica de Arte Cubano with the news. No one believed him. The cops in the street wanted to kick his dissident foreign ass, and the few people who knew were acting like my mother, watching the action unfold or wandering around the streets.

Pamela and I didn't cry big fat tears or make big opposition speeches—we didn't feel ready. We were sad because the theater had been closed for a while and because my mother had a really intense seizure that night, and that was basically all I could think about.

Gérard assumed we hadn't drunk or smoked in a week, but Pamela and I had smoked and drunk enough for all of Cuba. In this privately owned restaurant, they serve us beers with the excuse that they're allowed to sell booze to foreigners. Our waitress eyes Gérard suggestively. Gérard eyes Pamela like she's an exotic fruit. I read the menu and think how it's undignified for anything to cost this much.

I order an extravagant dish, the same one as Pamela. Gérard orders fish filet. A little toast to hide my sadness and guilt. A little playing dumb, which always goes over well at these kinds of lunches. Gérard is super involved with young artists: He wants us to tell him about trendy projects and use trendy words, he's always trying to find ways to connect things and ideas, he listens giddily and seems willing to collaborate. I like that. I picture him naked. I know he's not going to notice me, but I like picturing him this way, living out a passage of Reinaldo Arenas's *Hallucinations*.

Even better, half-naked. Half-naked and a bit of a dupe for believing in our projects, for believing in progress on earth, for being so moronic. Half-naked, moronic Gérard wants to show off his good taste to us. How will we move forward, Gérard? I have no intention of moving. I want to be transported somewhere else, then sit there until it's all over. That's what I want, Gérard, inertia.

The waitress looks like someone out of a classic telenovela, one of those low-budget soaps broadcast on Cuban television that make everyone in the country so dumb, it's all anyone can talk about, like those K-dramas my sister orgiastically laps up. I guess a pink tongue is the tongue that's obliged to talk and serve us a contrived smile that reminds me how contrived my body feels every time I have sex. The best thing I can do is have sex with strangers and not say a single word—it resets the body.

Gérard knows that Pamela and I still have some brains left. We complain, and we have down-and-out lives, but we also have the illusion that our miserable progress toward nowhere isn't really real—it's just a transition. It's nice to picture him naked. Lovely. Especially since he's a spiritual person, a critical thinker, and he knows about the larval underside of our culture and also the precarious system that upholds it. He wants to support us because he sees us smiling and looking committed and sad as we get things done under the radar. Let's do it. A stage performance based on the letters of Julián del Casal and Gustave Moreau. Gérard is taken with the idea. Gérard would trade this meal for the opportunity to eat Pamela's ass. Just the thought of it probably makes him relish the taste in his mouth.

I want to stage a version of Sartre's *The Respectful Prostitute*, but they want something more poetic. For my part, I can get behind anything after a couple of beers, and there's nothing sadder than Julián del Casal, who never had a chance at happiness.

So Gérard smiles. By the time the waitress brings the bill, we're drunk, mixing one thing with another and spouting nonsense about music. Gérard finds it hilarious, what will people on the street think now that we're wasted and they're not, what will they think looking at us walking to Vapor 69 after ingesting enough yeast to swell our stomachs and leave us bloated with the privilege of being treated like foreigners.

Pamela and I are keeping busy with two nineteenth-century artists, not the twentieth-century politician who died in peace in the twenty-first century, something not all politicians have been fortunate enough to achieve—a peaceful death. In some ways, my grandfather didn't die in peace. Bit by bit, his sluggish year-long death ate away at his life and his personality. This is the last time I'll see Gérard. I don't know this in the moment, but I do now. Now I know that this is the last time Pamela and I will speak with him and that there will be no play or world tour, which he himself had suggested. Pamela and Gérard will see each other again, and things will get weird. Around this table, I was always the fly, the meddlesome whore.

Pamela and I start walking. It's like a two-hour walk back to her house, but we don't have money for a car and we're in no state to take the bus. To be honest, we're wasted and a little worried and the mess with Mayuli's place was meant to scare us (I'd only just realized I had an imaginary relationship with that space). We share a vague idea of peril. As my mother would put it, we never consider the consequences, we don't know how to judge for ourselves what destiny awaits us because our generation behaves like parasites.

I don't know why I've barely thought about it, I really don't, it's as if Mayuli doesn't exist to me, as if I could gather everything I ever felt for him into a single thought and then go to the police station to save him.

That was the night I met Jara. Finally, something delightful.

Pamela didn't like Jara at first, but Jara yanked me out of limbo.

Jara isn't a weasel. She's a woman with the most musical name in all of Cuba, a woman who appreciates long silences and infectious laughter at parties, and despite her appreciation, she keeps her eyes open. Jara, the editor. Jara, the knower.

We meet her at the house of a cinematographer who's throwing a secret party. There she is. Her hair's loose and she seems super relaxed, full of this, I don't know, happiness that makes her easy to talk to. Pamela blurts out that she's corny, but I see something I like. What would Simone de Beauvoir have to say about my behavior, my brain, my sex? She'd feel sorry for me, for sure. Jara looks at me with sorry eyes.

Gérard: He's a colonizer. A colony is a by-product of syringes and sugar. Coloniality is when you wear down a country that's always belonged to someone else, it's when you wear down a moral product, a prevailing ideology, a certain neocolonial cycle that started with extermination and is now being upheld by weasels. I like colonizers who pay for lunch. Their mediocre rhetoric. Their communist ideas over caviar. I like colonizers whose brains are bathed in ideals. They arrive in the country wanting to decolonize their own ignorance. I like the joy and innocence with which colonizers make you feel unintelligent, a dreg, a kind of ritual record of this outdated sense of belonging to a place where every minor change feels colonial, where love is colonial, and grief. Gérard can break all the rules because he's a colonizer. My mother and I dwell in the underworld of sweet nothings, which we also share with the weasels, who are oblivious to how literal they are. We are from the commune of the nothings. Gérard is going to get Pamela out of this country. He told her so at the table: If you want to leave Cuba, I can get you a residency in Paris. In that moment, I knew what was coming and what would be left behind. No, it was already clear we'd never put on the play about the French painter who didn't understand the Cuban poet's love. We'd met Gérard at Humboldt just a few weeks ago. We'd talked to him about art until he left with a light-skinned, curly-haired jabaíto who danced beautifully. That night, Pamela hadn't paid any attention to him.

Censorship. Censorship begins with a subject, and it ends with death. An overly penetrating logic of underdevelopment and corruption. This week, as the weasels take center stage with their mourning, I'd like to defecate in their censor-mouths.

None of them helped me take my mother to the hospital. One suggested, in his illiteracy, that I put a spoon in her mouth. Another one assured me that pressing a hot knife to the back of her head would kill the seizure. My mother, turned weasel. My shuttered theater. Let the weasels have the theater, let them have the poetry, let them have the decisions. For a long time now they've been the ones saying "homeland," "epilepsy."

I've gotten into the habit of waking up with pessimistic ideas knocking around in my head.

Yaneika told me: "You're too pessimistic. Life lasts a second and then it's over, mi niña. You should make the most of the long life you've got ahead of you."

Alberto, with his death, told me: "This is a bottomless pit. We'll slash our throats in the sports field. We'll be left with the aftertaste of impossible love, because the only thing after this is death, and no one likes death."

The play we were staging at the theater was about a camp full of stateless people, an agricultural labor camp designed by the Cuban government. Families or individuals who wanted to travel to the United States, on direct flights departing from Varadero, had to do forced labor at those camps while waiting for their turn. It was the closest thing to a prison, to a panopticon, to miserable weasel domination tied to the "uniformity," the "concentration," and the "provisionality" of everything thought to be hard and soft.

I've never really understood what's so social about indoctrination—it's an inherently human trait. The bodies treated like beasts of burden are slowly executed. The lives treated like chess pieces are eliminated and then promptly forgotten. I don't want to think about how my mother felt when they censored the play and shut down the theater, because the only thing my mother ever thinks is that I'm a huge disappointment to her and all doctrines that are beautiful and good.

Maybe that's why she has seizures, because she's scared for me and my future, maybe I'm her illness and that's why none of her tests showed an epileptic focus.

At least they didn't put us through an act of repudiation or blow things out of proportion. They just released us and said: "Find something better to do than staging a hissy fit about the past. Your theater will now be undergoing major renovations. Your little works of art too."

The tongue went dark and the ears oozed a dark paste and the sex dripped dark blood. The weasels have the power to turn everything dark, even love. But that's Pamela's turn of phrase, I think. She's the playwright, not me—she's the one with a gift for words, not me. I'm just a set designer who thinks the world can be grasped by reading a few books and taking a critical look at power, a set designer with a lot of pessimism and virtually no control over what her body wants.

Censorship does not reach my teenage sister's ears. My sister, whose first time was at a José Martí Pioneers Camp, and who came home from that place half-asleep: She doesn't know that I know the secret of her virginity. In fact, I keep trying to forget it out of respect for her convenient assimilation into this world we've invented.

My sister's mouth was reddish, and she'd covered her marks on the way to the shower, covering something up with every step, as if she were hiding the patriotic value of her body, a fourteen-year-old girl who'd come home different, confused in a way that frightened me. But I didn't say anything. I just looked at her and remembered how lonely I'd felt the day someone filled a room with rose petals and put on this terrible Chayanne song, and I lay back on the bed with my legs spread open wondering if it was worth the wait and if there was any point in doing it again.

When my sister came home from camp I was waiting for her so that we could sleep in each other's arms.

Whatever. We're not all girls dreaming about our first time. Not all of us are eleven-year-olds who love our pillows and learn to rub ourselves into consciousness. I think I'm already tired, even though I haven't lived, even though I haven't resisted or struggled. Let the weasel come here and maim me, I don't care.

The first time at UMAP, the Military Units to Aid Production. The first time cutting sugarcane and sowing taro. The first time we yelled "Scum!" at our enemies. The first egg in the first hand. Now they have flowers and dark hats. The animal has died, and all I feel is a little sorry, or I don't know what I feel, because I can never figure out if what I perceive is consistent or just a scowl reverberating inside me. I pull faces, I pull glowering faces for photos held in private collections.

Mayuli told me censorship is like getting a plate of food and picking out the seasoning with your fingers—negating the recipe, in a way, and showing disgust for the meal you've been served. But Mayuli says there's always some trace left: The dish was prepared with those spices and there's no way to really hide the flavor.

I head to a Wi-Fi park to write.

"Is this a camp for stateless people?"

"Wi-Fi card."

"Girl, do you want a Wi-Fi card?"

"Girl, are you a friki or a dyke?"

The weasels don't enter here. The time I was censored doesn't enter here. Mosquitoes do not enter here. Snack vendors do not enter here. People come to this place to exorcize his death and celebration. A parade, a chorus of voices, the sun, and a family reunion reduced to a phone screen. The things we tend to. Crying and not crying. People yelling and people whispering. Send me money. Send me those pink shoes. Send me a pic. They speak through their absence: In the face of this spectacle of life, what is there in the death of a man? I want to disappear.

Everyone in this park has logged on to the Wi-Fi. They voice their sorrows. An old woman sits down next to me. I don't have money for a Wi-Fi card, so I'm just sitting here, just sitting and thinking about what a drag Centro Habana is without music. But I'm like this city, this neighborhood—I'll let anyone possess me, and not only on Sundays. My mother wanders around with her briefcase visiting houses and pressuring people to join the march, the official mourning, the great event. My mother sprinkles a little Abate on my plate every day, hoping I'll change.

If I let a weasel touch me, do I become a weasel? The first weasel? The first stone? Is there a parallel reality where no one censors anyone and you can just be happy? Is there a parallel reality where Mayuli isn't in prison? Is there a parallel reality where I'm not also stateless? Is there another dimension where our play did get staged?

In a way, it's a good thing my father left me—I'm the black sheep, the epitome of what a woman, a mother, an indoctrinated person has to carry, an embarrassment for the CDR, an object of suspicion among the weasels.

I'll stay in the camp for stateless people. I want to have a good time in these idle festivities. Crackled eyes. Eyes seeping dark drool. Dark is a state of mind. Dark is the dissolution of this time.

The weasels are surviving—and not through honesty but with killer instinct. Who censors who? What? Weasel?

We said nothing. We let ourselves be mauled by the army of weasels. People shout in the same trashy way they always have in the hallway outside our little room in Centro Habana. The same trashiness we get from Pirandello's thousand masks. Foucault wouldn't have had anything to say about this. Today I won't do anything but write a play. I'm not sure what play yet, whether it's going to be about emigration or the photos of Operation Peter Pan, when hundreds of children were transported in shoeboxes on planes.

"Where are these kids going? Will they come back?"

"When are you coming?"

"Will you be back?"

They ask and ask and ask, everyone is always asking someone when they're coming back, and if they're not asking, then they're writing, they're probably writing all the time. When will you be back? When we ask about a return, what we're really asking about is forgetting. I get the sense we're all scared of being abandoned—the censors, the starving masses, the weasels—scared of the drought, the emptiness, of switching colonies. I'm scared to death.

My philosopher boyfriend and Mayuli share an impressive capacity to define everything.

I woke up with the urge to write, but since I'm a designer I won't write anything. I'm just going to sit here, listening to other people, letting time pass, smoking this cigarette I got from Gérard, exhausted and sipping pesticide, hoping to throw up or die so that Mayuli will listen to me and not think I don't care about what he's going through. I didn't sleep on Saturday. The guy died, which happens—everyone does. The meter reader brought my mother a whole chicken.

I think about her, about Jara. We had an amazing time together. She helped me forget my disgust toward R. She had a copy of *Breach of Trust* in her backpack—it was so weird seeing those words in her backpack. Apparently she's researching Ángel Escobar. Everything feels light with her. Maybe she's the reason I had the urge to write.

Her mouth is a kind of half-open shell. A smell of dulce de leche floats out from inside and is immortalized in my nose. Something about her legs turns me on like a photo by Ren Hang—must be the paleness I glimpse on her thighs. The smell of a mouthful of dulce de leche, and the taste of pale skin concealed from the sun. I've never thought about nudity in the vein of that philosopher who my boyfriend hated but I loved, Giorgio Agamben, because I was raised on pornographic postcards and got turned on by everything. Nudity as a loss of innocence. Nudity as the death of innocence. And her free legs in a freedom frame of mind. Someone who's young and not a parasite like Pamela or me has legs like Jara. I still haven't gotten tired of looking at her legs, hypnotized by their whiteness and her powerful way of being uncommon.

I want to cut her hair. Opening a page at random, I play with the book in my hand as if it means something. She smiles because she knows Pamela and I arrived drunk at the photographer's party and that now there's no alcohol in my blood—I'm just myself, not the Manichean character of a pubescent artist with the same sense of style as everyone else and the same topics of conversation.

She looks at me like I'm a gecko trying to get away from her. She says I must be an actress, and I know that's not what she's trying to tell me.

"I'm not an actress, I'm a set designer."

"Boring."

"Not a set designer, a playwright."

"Boring."

"I'm not anything."

We smoke. Things start flowing. She has this air of not being totally from here, and it saves her, saves her from disappearing in a crowd. I'd like to find another way of feeling—to feel the way I feel now, but most of the time, to feel light, to feel light constantly, enveloped in lightness. I don't know if it's the absence of light and savageness that gives rise to this mediocre state of survival, or if this mix is the breath that gets the weasels going in this week of patriotic hammering. Time is busy sating hunger: *Going on a walk* or *making love* are simple phrases that point to a lifestyle that doesn't belong to us, posing just isn't what we do, Mayuli would say.

After I smoke a little something, I get political and start talking shit. My philosopher boyfriend talks a lot of shit—he got me into the habit, and it comes out when I write and think.

Fierce, savage weasels standing in line for fried chicken. Human, deprived weasels like me who let themselves be shaken by the masses, who let themselves be written by others, who stand at the end of the line to buy who the hell knows what. Weasels in the Plaza de la Revolución. I lock myself in a room with a weasel and weep.

They're saying there won't be concerts or music for a long time. What release valve will they drum up for our thirsty citizens. What will the weasels feed on during all these ceremonious farewells. Societies of weasels have taught us that the notion of satisfaction breaks our spirits and gags us. I don't know any other society but this one. A society that bans *The Hard and Soft* is a society of weasels.

Jara doesn't get why I keep manhandling her book and pretending to be a connoisseur of Ángel Escobar and singing the praises of her research subject and going on and on about the details of his life. I suspect that these biographical facts represent a writer I don't know and would like to know better. She also doesn't get my weaselly definitions of contemporary Cuba; she doesn't get my tangents, my dissent.

I keep my feelings about her legs to myself—I haven't completely lost it yet. She's a little shy, but between the red shirt she has on and those legs, it isn't hard to picture her in a Ren Hang portrait. I could ask her to put on the needle corset, but carefully so she doesn't get pricked. Paint her nails red and suck her nipple with lips also painted red. Red against a white bed. Red against a flowery bed. Red. Reddish lightness. Leaving red lipstick on her breasts.

I let myself be swept up in the routine provisionality of mating rituals, fulfilling the pattern of male-on-male domination. As we talk, all the lessons I've learned fail again and again. With her, everything is different. Here we are, the two of us, and even though I'm spouting crap from a dusty old script, I start feeling like myself, totally light, talking to her without feeling guilt or having to act like a little lady. Here we are, the two of us, stoned, sitting in a park.

I'm going to have to find a job, something that doesn't involve sleeping with an old man, being used like a rag, or being a lost cause. Pamela and I wanted to write a play so that we could go on tour, evade the censors, but the truth is we got used to wasting time. Pamela and I found a way to secretly be weasels, although weasels know what they are and we don't. Being aware, learning to be aware.

I wanted to tell her about R, I wanted her to feel sorry for me and worry about my mental health, for her to save me. I wanted to tell her about Pamela, Mayuli, Alberto, about my grandfather—all this was going through my head while I looked at her. Tell her about my mother's job and how I filmed her fucking the meter reader. Show her every perverse corner of me. I wanted to put true horror in front of her and have her still want me. Actually, what I wanted was to tell her every single thing about my life so that she would get scared and leave behind the chaos inside me.

A text from Pamela interrupts us. She says that Jara and I have nothing to talk about, that I should quit this crap with her, that I'm not into girls. She warns me that she got a summons. The cops want to know what goes on in Mayuli's room. They're going to send me a summons too. They know I've smoked there, that I've slept with people there, and I know it's illegal. I can't tell Jara. My happy afternoon is stalled, and everything goes back to the usual pointless shitty logic. I'm stateless in my own reality. I'm in limbo. We agree to meet again at Malecón and Paseo. I hope it doesn't rain. This is the best afternoon I've had all year.

Mayuli: They ask him why he does it, and the young man says it's a way to make a little money, but he only rents the place to upstanding couples. They ask about the drugs. He says they're right, there are drugs. The minute he does this he knows he shouldn't have been so frank. Why does he do this. Why doesn't he go to school. Why does he live alone. Mayuli says he is a child prodigy, that he doesn't need to go to school because you don't need a degree in the streets, what you need is to know how to laugh in the face of the government. As he says this, they assume that the young man already knows what awaits him. Mayuli isn't kidding around—he doesn't want anything anymore. It's not cheek, or sass, or an anarchic interrogation performance piece—he's simply known what his fate would be ever since they asked for his reasons. The only thing left is for him to have a good time.

The pictures on our apartment walls. The pictures my mother makes an effort to get printed and framed. They end up looking sad, those pictures. People walk into your house and look at them, then feel sorry for you and your mother's wretched attempts at protection.

Here, in this country, we enjoy being consumed by the nostalgia of a moment trapped in amber. We are collectors of our own lives, of what our lives-on-display should say about us. We like to hang pictures and show off our photo albums and say we're happy because there are photos of us standing behind a cake hugging and smiling. The collection of the vanquished, that's what it should be called, the collection of vanquished weasels, the photogenic nature of simple things.

The Wolf won't stop texting me. *Little Red Riding Hood, I'm ready for more*, he says, and even though the bruise on my arm has faded, I can't think of a single reason to go to his house. That's one thing I like about my arrangement with R, no matter how sick and depraved it may be. We see each other on Sundays, and after that my life has nothing to do with our meeting. But this macho, with his direct messages—*he's* the stalker type, a machofucker who wants to turn me into his woman-object, his plaything. There's something sublime in his backwoodsy behavior, something tender in his coarseness, or maybe it's just me, sugarcoating everything, like a true daughter of this proliferation, a loser. I don't reply.

I'm in my Ren Hang phase, which you could also call my Jara phase. Since I don't have a job or a theater, I'm drawing sketches of her white legs inspired by the work of the banned Chinese photographer. The sadness of his photographs is like the sadness of a lightning strike, like the sadness of the pictures on the walls of our apartment in Centro Habana, which are obviously sadder and more pornographic. I've been writing again too, though I'll never top *The Hard and Soft*, so instead I write for the immutability of the day.

When my mother has a seizure, she has my heart in her mouth and in her animal groans, but then she goes out to join the weasels. My mother should've posed for a melancholic Chinese photographer like me. My mother says Ren Hang's work is pornographic and I'd better keep my sketches away from my sister, my sister who visits her boyfriend during his military service and swallows military dick as proof of her love. My mother doesn't read my sister's diaries, but I do. I read everything I find, and everything I read makes up my own personal collection: "Vas bien, hija, vamos bien." You're doing fine, hija, we're doing fine.

Pamela got a summons at her house yesterday. Pretty soon I'll get mine. In hindsight, I've only been to Mayuli's place twice, and we didn't smoke—I've never smoked there. The first time we went over for a bite to eat because we were starving, and the second there was a group of us and we were already fucked up, I only have flashes of what happened, everyone on top of each other, buckets of sweat, I remember following a cockroach on the floor with my eyes, wanting to touch it but not being able to. I remember it hurt but also that it was a relief.

All this reminds me of when I was arrested with my friend E. E was my best friend in undergrad, but she left the country and blocked me on Facebook with no warning. The thing that's most pathetic about the virtual world is that I don't recognize her in her photos, though I pretend to, I pretend I'm seeing her, that we're still together. We were with these Argentinians who'd come to the Havana Theatre Festival, and we were the guides for the group. What actually happened is that we fell in love with two of the actors and became their girlfriends on day one.

We fled La Habana for Varadero. We had the worn-out look of classic art students, simple, kind of snobby, but also enthusiastic and hippyish. We could pass for anything but jineteras—we were kind of sorry-looking, just like our street-theater Argentinian boyfriends with their flip-flops and disheveled backpacker looks. Our plan was to camp on the sand in Varadero and sleep in each other's arms.

A couple of cops arrested us for solicitation. The Argentinians wanted to take a stand against authority, but the officers wouldn't listen. They took all four of us to the police station for disrupting the peace. We were about to be fined when E broke into tears and showed them her Young Communist League card. We told them about how we went to ISA, how there was a theater festival in Havana, and how we'd started dating those starving Argentinians who did street theater.

That police station is still the filthiest place I've ever been. The station and the military area where the boy I dated as a teen did his pre-training, that's where I experienced some of the foulest, most painful smells I've ever encountered. My sister is already familiar with one of them—I've never been able to protect her from anything. It's not that she wants my protection, only that she needs to feel less alone.

If I get called to testify against Mayuli, I'll have to act dumb and cry like E cried that time. I don't want to spend the night in jail because of a few tokes, it's not that big a deal, I don't know anything about what goes on in that little room. They've got their eye on young people who are off the rails. I'm not in the mood for cop stuff. I am in my immutability, and that's the absolute truth—observing and sketching photographs, chill. But if they summoned Pamela, then they're going to summon me, since we're the same, I'm sure they're going to summon me. Though, to be honest, Pamela went to Mayuli's nearly every day. Maybe I can tell them R is my uncle and get them to call him and ask about me, yeah, that's what I'll do, let the old letch make himself useful. I'll give them his name and number. I picture his face when he answers the call, his sick military officer's anger and guilt. But I bet he won't feel embarrassed, just proud of his naughty domesticated girl. I'd be his moral trophy, a cockroach that he follows with his eyes and reaches for whenever he wants.

Our apartment is a museum of faces. The first thing I will ban if I ever have a place of my own is pictures on walls. Photos are artifacts, they say, and to me they look like grimaces that speak of death, of the one thing that's outside any and all collections: life. Taking pictures has become very democratic, but the excitement of going to a photography studio shouldn't have died such a sudden death. Photos are fine—it's the invasion of family pictures on walls that's the problem. The accumulation of moments, of the fiction of family, of family history, of the desire to keep experiencing something we can't even identify anymore.

I am so bored. . . My sister isn't bothered by the dirty old man poems in her pink diary. She actually appreciates that I copied them out for her, probably because she assumes it's the only act of love I'm capable of. There's nothing fake about those poems, unlike my life, our life, where everything is superficial. Boredom and laziness, a healthy lifestyle, smoking and sorting rice if and when I'm asked—there's nothing for me to do besides think about those white legs. I hope they don't put Mayuli away for good, that would be the end of so much, I don't know, I hope nothing happens to him. When I watch my sister sleep, it makes me so sad, she's nothing like me, she knows how to be happy, which is why I try not to show her anything.

The TV continues to bombard us with propaganda, and my mother continues to wait for the meter reader. The *Aedes aegypti* heroine is sick, but the little things still make her happy. A liturgy of the muck I'm not ready for. I'm not in mourning. It's my moment, the shipwreck, limbo, the black hole, the redness, the dog of boredom. It's a fizzling-out in the void while I wish I could wash away all my disgust at the cut-up photos.

My grandfather is the only man I've ever mourned. My only wistful memories are of him, the rest either make me sick or make me rot or make me suffer. That's it, if I get summoned, I'm going to tell them to call R. It's been two days of complete, glorious silence, and I miss Jara, who hasn't written to me since yesterday. We'd agreed to meet at Malecón and Paseo. She doesn't see anything lovely in me, only a Little Red Riding Hood with a deformed vocabulary and an artist's spirit. She shouldn't look at all those frames hanging on my wall. It's probably disheartening enough for her to see me so lost, camouflaged behind words and personal effects. Pictures are also a kind of personal effect. Maybe it's not a good time to start something, maybe someone told her stuff about me and Pamela. Maybe Mayuli was being watched, and if he was, well, we're the only ones who go everywhere with him.

Little Red Riding Hood, you're still playing cat and mouse. Lemme at you. He doesn't realize that I was only with him because I'm lazy and dying and because I enjoy the self-indulgence that comes from not having desires, not having real desires, from seeing the roof of his house as my only shelter. I went to him because I wanted to exorcize politics in his arms, but I don't care anymore, none of this says anything about my stupidity anymore. Having your waist squeezed too hard and your nipples sucked too enthusiastically is a little invasive. And the Revolution has invaded my house more than enough for me to have to put up with this crap about how things are better when they're more intense. It's a myth. What I want is to let myself go. Like one of those Ren Hang kisses that are so sad they exonerate you from your commonness. Like one of those girl kisses Jara gave me that I'm hoping to get again.

There's nothing I can do. Except acquire a taste for drawing across from the wall that holds my mother's collection. Except acquire a taste for making sketches parading as drawings parading as self-portraits parading as a design for a censored play or for a play with the financial backing of a colonizer named Gérard. And even though these drawings serve no purpose, there's nothing I can do except think about how it's good to be inspired by facts again, to selfishly forget Mayuli, to do nothing for Mayuli, to do nothing besides wait for Sunday to come.

My life without photos. There isn't a single photo of me at Humboldt.

My mother is on the floor. Needle in my hand. I can't move. Drool. Tongue. Teeth. Shoulders. Elbows. Fingers. My mother is on the floor. I can't hold her up.

Mayuli: I fell in love with you and always felt scared of you too. I think we went to the same elementary school and packed the same snack every day: bread with oil and salt. I remember people made fun of us, but that didn't hurt me; no one has ever been able to hurt me, nothing has ever hurt me more than being useless, than striving to be useless. I knew you had a crazy uncle, the guy who jerked off at the school window, but I didn't tell you that either. I didn't tell anyone. I don't want you to suffer, not over anything. But it looks like things are going to end the way they began, bad things are going to happen, I have this feeling, even though it doesn't hurt me. I've known it since we sat together in the back of the classroom, I've known since then that something bad would happen to you. Then we didn't see each other again, you forgot we were ever at the same school, you forgot the birthdays, and the pictures with the bandanas. I will never forget your uncle's face, he made sure we'd never forget it.

All I want is for you to be okay.

Everyone's talking about the same thing, about how Mayuli made money selling drugs. How he got involved with everything in the room on Humboldt, and how everything surrounding the room is shit. Which is really difficult, because they shoved Pamela against the wall, and what was she supposed to do? Pamela's weak, Sunday at the police station, waking up there in the morning. The cops can't lock you up for smoking weed at someone's house. There's something else going on, and they want to get to the bottom of it.

My mother has constant headaches. It isn't normal for her to have another seizure so close to the last one. She's sad, everything in her world is crumbling to pieces, she doesn't know what she loves—the meter reader, or her country, or her off-the-rails daughter, who was once the family's pride and joy. My dad and I must've been the family's pride and joy. They slipped a summons under the door, my sister is crying, my sister's boyfriend hugs her. He passed his military service, he came back thin and ghostly, he looks like a dummy version of the boy he used to be. A family tragedy layered over a political tragedy. Jara invited me out for ice cream, I need to leave behind this state of immutable chaos.

Jara takes me to a new place where they sell gelato, and I have gelato for breakfast. All kinds of businesses have popped up over the last few years. There are weasels in this country with money, photogenic weasels with dinero.

She has this odd way of smiling, like her smile is always falling, which reminds you of the fleetingness of laughter—you don't want it to end, but you know it will, and suddenly. I don't really know what it is that's making me laugh, but I'm smiling like a maniac, and I spill the ice cream all over me. She seems lighter than ever, pointing with her finger at the dribble of cold dairy on my shirt. I tell her about the theater and the Alexander McQueen shows I have saved on my hard drive. She doesn't judge me. She doesn't judge me now and she won't later, just smiles.

I'm going to look for that Egon Schiele painting. It's a portrait of the past. Before Jara even existed, there was another model with her same silhouette, her lightness. We walk to La Playita de 16, I don't know why I've never gone to that beach before. That's where the big concrete structures are, the ones that look like a pile of oversized aquatic scatter jacks—they've always given me a weird feeling. There are three lost dogs roving along the coast. I think of dogs as spirits that also get lost. Jara goes up to the dogs, pets them, the three dogs mill around her feet, and I cry, tears slipping from my eyes.

"You look like one of Egon Schiele's models."

"You think?"

"I think of that painting when I look at you. I'm going to set it as my background."

"Why don't you give the painting to me?"

"We could go to your place."

"I'm busy this afternoon. I'll call you tomorrow."

Jara walks in a relaxed way, and the dogs follow us.

I don't think I've ever had that thing people call a destiny. I move in a lot of directions but none of them are my destiny. They're just distances, sudden detours, like now, I don't feel anything for her or the dogs, I'm just moving in that direction, which is no direction, and I get tired thinking of my mother with so much hatred, my mother who probably feels like those dogs. I don't know myself.

I'm busy this afternoon too. My mother is busy recovering.

He's desperate today. R is desperate. He wants me to down the tea, he doesn't want to listen to my chatter, he doesn't look at me. I know he's acting weird, he doesn't want to talk, he looks down on me, but all I can think about is his teeth. I stare at his dentures, he's so ridiculous it's a relief.

I drink all the tea.

R on the floor. Legs splayed open. He smells like damp wood and dried sweat. He smells of piss. His teeth are gone, his tongue black. There's a kilo of powder on the nightstand. I'd never seen any cocaine there before. I'm not dizzy, I just feel a little slow. All of a sudden it's cold. All of a sudden the sun rises. It's not Schubert, though it sounds like it. If I had a knife, I could be Isabelle Huppert in *The Piano Teacher*. This is not a play, this is really happening. It wasn't a circus act. He's dead, and today I didn't press record on my phone. I open the nightstand drawer, palm all the money I can find, 380 CUC altogether, I don't have time to take anything else. To be honest, I'm not entirely sure why I take the money, I just don't know. I get up, blubbering, but I move on autopilot, I immediately make a run for it.

I know I'm doing something wrong, I'm running away, leaving him there. It's called fleeing the scene of the crime, which is different from killing him, or I don't really know if I killed him, I don't know what I'm doing. It all lasted the length of a dream. I was with him and then suddenly I was waking up, exhausted, covered in blood and piss. It smells fucking vile, I get dressed, walk out of there as I am. But I'm running away, and I don't even know if he's really dead.

My mother is waiting for me, my mother is always waiting for me. I get there in tears, stinking. I put the money on the table. My mother is crying, she smacks me, shoves me, I don't want to see her like this, so weak, I don't want to see what I've pushed her towards, maybe it's me, maybe I'm the reason for the rot. The two of us are alone, and I tell her, for the first time I tell her what was going on with R. She tells me we have to go to his house, then asks if any of his neighbors saw me and says not to mention the money.

"Get in the shower. Shower, then we'll go."

My mother won't stop crying. She coughs. Hands me a towel. My mother isn't exhausted or beaten down by her seizures. She puts me in the shower. I can't stop crying. It's as if I'm reliving the pain I felt when my grandfather died, the pain of a son or daughter dying, the pain of my dead enjoyment draped over a table where I am penetrated by hundreds of men who claim to know me and what I want and need.

We run over there. Everything happens so fast, we go to R's house. We can't get in. Standing on the street, my mother calls an ambulance. My hair is wet, it's impressive how quickly my hair has grown. Weasels everywhere, staring at me, judging me. My mother isn't ashamed. She stands with me at the door.

They break down the door. It's all happening now. I ask the cop for a cigarette, and he doesn't understand how I have the gall to ask him for a cigarette. Meanwhile, I don't understand if he's looking at me with disgust or pity or something like sadistic desire. My mother tells me to shut up. I think of my grandfather's dead embrace. If Jara saw me now, she'd reject me wholesale, because there's nothing in me that could be useful to her.

The sun rises, and I'm at the police station. There are security cameras all over R's house. They don't say anything about the money. They're studying the evidence. Apparently he died of natural causes. No one mentions the cocaine.

Pamela sold her grandma's house. Inheritances are meant to be sold, that much I've learned. The weasels have inherited, by force, everything that we are. So many empty houses and mansions that belong to no one. Given everything going on with Mayuli, we won't be staging any performances with the money Gérard promised to scrape together. It'll be on hold forever.

How am I supposed to tell Jara that I can't meet her today because I'm at the police station in Centro Habana?

I'm tired of wearing myself out talking and talking and saying nothing, it must be a bad habit that weasels have— weasel archipelago, weasel philosopher, like the boyfriend I still miss sometimes because he really loved me.

My life as an archipelago, a bunch of islands connected in some way, apart but also sometimes touching. I don't know why the death of that old man hurt so much, it's like a part of me didn't want him to die, like I was hesitant to lose that flawed, dark, eternal archipelago. There, in his room, I was running from something more intense than his sexual assaults, I was running from the everyday ways I was broken: by theater, by lovers.

My mother is very quiet, mute. What are we supposed to do with this money that belongs to no one? And what about his house? I should've been more careful and tried to find whatever it was he put in that tea, saved a little for every Sunday.

When I was in high school, they called my mother in. According to the weasels, my behavior was aggressive, and I liked to "start little campaigns." One of our disgusting weasel teachers had raped my best friend. The principal threatened to expel me for falsely accusing a teacher and making a scene. My mother got to the school, glared at me. My friend said it was a lie, that I'd made the whole thing up. How the hell could I have made up the blood and dirty clothes, the bruises. After Alberto, I vowed never to stay silent, to rebel; after Alberto killed himself, I took up rebellion as a language of survival. Swallowing hard, like now, swallowing hard gulps of shit.

My mother has never managed to instill any discipline in me—this is what hurts her the most about her daughter. Now she feels sorry for me, she knows I'm a lost soul, that my "little campaigns" are nothing but mousy rebellions, that my hatred for weasels is nothing but a string of tantrums, that my violated body is like that of my high-school friend, and just now, in the police station, I've realized that nothing is too serious, nothing is immutable, everything happens lightly. My archipelagos, like a country, thrive on cycles of pain, their states of being do not come from authentic pain.

My mother doesn't mention the money, she is also my accomplice. It feels like this disaster will always be my backdrop. Before a court of guilty subjects, mea culpa. Before the false distribution of the world and of life and of pleasure, how I absolutely shit on everything I touch, my absolute uselessness. My mother is standing—now she sees everything.

The text Pamela sent yesterday: *They're taking away M's apartment, everything else too . . . His family's coming from Miami bc there's gonna be a trial. We're off the hook. xx.* Mayuli's arrest will be the end of a lot of things, but also the beginning of a widening limbo. Now that R is dead, I don't know what will happen to me. I see myself at every stage of my life reliving this guilt. I think of R's body looking at me. That's what will be left of his memory, another dead body to remember.

Dead weasel: Once the weasel dies, every minor detail becomes a memory of him. Remembering him in surfaces, in slogans, in the graphic and iconic memory of a Revolution. Remembering the meaninglessness of his life. Memories are not transcendental, every single element leaves a mark, no matter how grotesque—it stays. When a weasel dies, money is earmarked for a biopic to be made in his name. The weasel that outlives the weasel is in charge of tending to the majestic biography of the weasel. This is when I begin to live—now, for the first time, I do my best to forget. The weasel is dead, and there's nothing left to silence.

They're reopening the theater. Of course, no one talks about *The Hard and Soft*, no one accepts the weaselfication of culture that caused this catastrophe. Now we're staging *Richard III*. I get a message from the manager, who used to be my philosopher, my boyfriend, telling me that we're all meeting at the theater on Wednesday to plan the work ahead of us.

At the police station they sit me down in a chair. Beside me, they're watching something on TV. I can't see the screen, but I recognize the sound: it's the same as the recordings I made with my phone. I recognize the scene, the nightstand, the mirror over the dresser. The wood, the smooth floor snapping, my skull cracking. I'm sure that the video sounds just like the recording on my phone. The cops touch each other openly, I can feel them caressing themselves while thinking about the mess I'm in.

Finally, one of them asks: "Do you know what this is?" I don't answer. "We're going to need some clarification." He isn't surprised, he speaks calmly, but I'm in trouble,

I haven't got out of the trouble I was already in for sex work and drugs. "Do you know what the officers are looking at? Do you realize how much we're going to need you to clarify? Start talking. Tell me everything, and I'll make things easy for you. Tell me about Humboldt first, and don't leave anything out. Tell me about your little friend. We'll come back to the video after. Things are looking complicated for you. You're mixed up in some filthy stuff. I mean, does your mother even know? I bet you don't have a dad, because if you did you wouldn't have so little self-respect. We've got some time here to try to understand the situation. Humboldt, your videos. How long have you known Mayuli?"

The rest of them are in the adjoining room, I can tell from the sounds. The one interrogating me says again: "Prostitution." And it's like I'm sitting at the movie theater, watching a film about my life without rhyme or reason.

The torture lasts two days. They insist I express something shameful and terrifying: They ask about Pamela, they ask about my mother and my friends, about the theater, about Gérard, but they never ask about R. I stick to the facts. They don't ask one question about the money, they never mention the 380 CUC. I don't remember any details from the interrogation, question after question, non sequiturs, what makes their questioning Cuban is that anything goes, they ask whatever pops into their minds, and they don't want to hold me, but my answers are bland and vague, they describe the facts and nothing more.

"R is like family."

They laugh, they jeer, at first quietly and then loudly, very loudly, crowded around the television where they lap up my reality TV show. A huge party kicks off at the police station. The male weasel walks in, breathes in and out, squeals, then sinks his teeth into my neck. The male weasel laughs, decides I'm innocent. I scream. The male weasel does not scream, he just breathes in and out, but his breathing is a complaint, the way he breathes is acrobatic, athletic, sexual. Now it looks like I'm the founding member of a film club. Everyone at the station is sending each other my audio files. Patrol shifts are no longer uneventful, long, tedious. My mother is the only one here for me.

At the entrance to the police station, my mother says, "R is like family."

They tell my mother: "Your daughter isn't here."

On the street I meet a very dirty man in a ripped sweater. He's rail-thin. I don't know why I stare at that man with a miserable, hypocritical look on my face, just like the weasels'. The guy recognizes the shitty look I give him. He's the first man in Cuba to perceive everything I'm thinking and feeling, which is why he's more generous than I am when he keeps walking, when he looks at the marks on my skin and keeps walking because he knows exactly what they are.

I make it to the meeting on Wednesday. Apparently the week is over, and my face is the clear-cut image of failure and the humiliation of hundreds of historic weasels; after the death, after their deaths, two months pass. And I forget every last detail. I lose my phone, forget the sounds. I never take the street by the police station, though I'm sure the patrol cars slow down to laugh at me.

Pamela, Pamela's gone.

Death is a deaf reflection, an MRI that can't detect the epileptic focus.

Jara writes to me every afternoon, she waits for me at the back door to the theater and kisses my forehead as if my forehead were pure, wholesome, as if it didn't sweat buckets, as if theater mites were good for you. Jara likes the designs I did for the play, she went with me to choose the fabric and also gave me a couple of literary critiques. I laugh a lot with her, sometimes I think she knows everything about Mayuli being in prison, about the trial I was never called to testify at, about Sundays with R, sometimes I think she can picture something, that she's hinting at something. I don't reply. Jara takes it upon herself to be like the pillow between my legs, the first point of contact with my vulva, the first demonstration of love. Pamela is gone. I don't know when in those two months Pamela left. She didn't go to the meeting that Wednesday, and we didn't see each other again.

My mother was committed last week after a really intense seizure. My sister and I held each other and fell asleep in the hospital room. The nurse sprained his leg hauling my mother—he didn't give a shit about my mother's heart—and my sister and I lunged at him like a pair of maniacs. In circumstances like these, you realize that there is an inexplicable sense of belonging in sharing fluids. I don't belong to my sister or my mother, I don't belong to anything except an evasive tea, an escape-hatch tea, a domineering weasel. Our misery is the washed-up love of three women who don't belong to each other. Though I do try to keep my sister from getting sullied by my life, because I love her like you wouldn't believe. My sister, who knows me and picks up on my reek, my sister, who's frightened by those two quiet, still months.

Now my mother is better, with her boyfriend, her papers, her patriotic little brochures, her circus, all of which keeps her going and saves her. My sister got bored of her boyfriend, no one knows what happened, but she's more relaxed now, more mature; I feel like she's gotten older and knows more about life than I do. She probably knows more about everything than I do—at least she knows more about why she behaves one way and not another, why she follows Mamá to all her patriotic campaigns, why she argues with her boyfriend and why, when she falls asleep beside her sister, she learns about the inevitable relationship between abandonment and death, between loneliness and sorrow. I, on the other hand, given all my choices, decided not to try to explain to myself the pain that's become entrenched in my family. Because we are women in a country of men.

Jara got me a job with a famous painter. I run errands for her and update her Facebook page, and I get a small salary in return, just enough to sustain a young, failed designer. Last week she asked me to design an invitation for her, and it dawned on me that maybe I could make a living from this. The pay isn't too bad, and it takes me no time at all. Yesterday I found some sketches for my Ren Hang-inspired drawing. Jara says they're good enough to be exhibited, that I should show them to the painter and ask if she can think of any use for them.

I'm on the hunt for a grant that will allow me to leave the country. Jara says we need to get away from the turbulence, and I'm trying to find an exit strategy. How do I get rid of this feeling that I have a dirty body? How do I get rid of this dirty weasel gaze? How do I ditch the habit of thinking of myself as disgusting, a piece of shit, a waste of space? How do I look at my perfect sister and not feel like I'm drowning in my own criticisms of this dead-end country? What will my sister inherit from me, what photos, family heirlooms, what weaselly chitters? Weasels running their tongues over my hair, which has grown longer over the past few months.

Jara is my only happy place. But I feel like I don't deserve her. I deserve to have my arm branded, my vagina stabbed, my memories wiped clean. I think the costumes for *Richard III* are going to look great. Plus, no one remembers *The Hard and Soft* anymore—it's like censorship doesn't even exist. Part of our education is shortening our long-term memory.

Jara doesn't like it when I smoke, so I don't smoke. She also doesn't like calling me Little Red Riding Hood. Instead she's christened me Surly Girl, because she says I like arguing with people on the street, even though I secretly despise that she calls me that, I feel like she's saying I'm a hater, but Jara can call me whatever she likes. Sometimes we get ice cream and walk long distances. Jara has taken Pamela's place, no one has taken R's, but they don't remember him either, just as they don't remember Fidel, they just parrot what they've been taught, that's what's Cuban about weaseldom. Jara and I walk, and she says my theory about the weasels is terribly exact: Everyone's a male weasel.

There is something too beautiful and pure in Jara. Sometimes she has a bit of a mean streak, but I've never been happier, so happy and so sad to be living right now.

"Can we start over?" I say to my sister in the hospital, our mother asleep beside us.

"It'll be exactly the same."

"The meter reader hasn't shown his face."

"He won't, he doesn't love her."

Mayuli is rotting in prison. Alberto is rotting in the school bathroom. R is rotting in his tomb for undefeated heroes. Jara and I are letting the decay of the ice cream cheer us.

"This hospital is in rough shape."

"I can't stand how damp hospitals are."

"It's inhumane."

My sister and I take our mother home. That night, we all sleep together. When we were still checked in at Cuerpo de

Guardia, Jara brought us ice cream. Yaneika is gone visiting her mother in Guantanamo, so she's not around to stroke our hair. All my mother wants is to eat ice cream. Melting ice cream.

Jara and I get to Coppelia, and we don't have to stand in line because we say we're going to Las Tres Gracias. I see an old man walking out and stop him. I tell him that Pamela and I took his notebook of poems. I say I have his poems at home, they're beautiful, and I want to give them back, that he's an amazing writer, he saved us that day. At first he says nothing, but I keep pushing, I keep pushing even though Jara doesn't understand what's going on.

"They're not mine. I copied them from somewhere."

He leaves slowly, hunched over, each step dragging with a mythical exhaustion. Life moves slowly and diligently treads the ground, the asphalt. When things happen, we feel like life is moving faster, but that isn't true, it's not events that give way to time, but loss, the possibility of exhaustion.

Jara doesn't understand. We're in luck, my mother is in luck—there's chocolate ripple ice cream.

My dear Pamela:

We'll probably stay friends after the cataclysm. A final act of rebellion that ends in the mummification of life and hope. I don't know if we'll ever get back our rebellious streak. I also don't know if we'll manage to live with this meaninglessness, this melancholy, with failure. Promise we'll be together and recapitulate this country that was never ours to begin with, the one that fit inside of Vapor 69. We'll remember some reggaeton song and a lover we shared.

I'll tell you about how I played Sleeping Beauty at the house of an old military officer, how I did exactly the same thing as that character in the movie you hated because the lead actor was not the person you wanted them to be: Like in a fairy tale, I drank the tea, then woke up to a loving kiss. Reality ended about the same way as fiction—no prince, no streamers, only silence.

The truth is I never told you about R because I wanted to keep our relationship separate from the Sundays I spent in complete limbo. The sole purpose of that secret arrangement was to serve as proof of my family's thick rot and despair.

I'm not sure where I picture you sitting while I write this letter. I think you'll always be freer than me because you're a writer and you can be happy anywhere there's another body and a balcony. When your grandma died, I thought you'd fall to pieces, and that's exactly why I'm so scared of you, because I know you're a whale, that you finally became a whale.

We never did write the play about Julián del Casal and Gustave Moreau, we never did it because instead we knew we'd have to make fun of Jean-Paul Sartre and Fidel Castro by staging a version of *The Respectful Prostitute*. That's the play I wanted to work on, a play about a whore who wasn't free because men never allow women to be free. *The Respectful Whore*.

We made the right choice to do nothing. In order not to become a weasel you have to do nothing, to live off of air, parties, and meaningless sex, to live off of despair. In order not to become a weasel, the only thing you can do is love.

When I write the word *love*, I think about how not everything has been low, sad, failed. Maybe I'll tell you about the biggest revelation I had. It was a dream, a dream about the poems by that old man in Coppelia. Do you remember? I swear I can't stop thinking about him. And I can't stop thinking about death either.

Do you think we were happy? Do you think we're happy now? The cataclysm has probably happened. You're my playwright. In my mind, we're sisters. You're the most beautiful woman I've ever known.

Sometimes I think I've been unfair to my mother. My mother always wanted me to be a writer, for me to get married and have kids. I think she liked the play you wrote for her, and in a way she felt like the hero in the campaign against the *Aedes aegypti* mosquito. I'm sure my mother wishes she had the same magical extermination powers as the protagonist of your play. She wants to use them to control the meter reader.

I don't blame you for anything, Pamela. All I want is for you to be happy, maybe married to a man from Greece or Lithuania, married with kids. . . There I go, echoing what my mother wants, what a dumbass. Recently, I found out I'm infertile. I can't have kids. I never told you, but I was pregnant once. I didn't tell you out of shame and anger and because of the clump of blood I saw disappear into a pile of waste at Emergencias hospital. This is also part of my story, my fairy tale, the death that floated around everything. My mother taught me to keep things quiet, and even though I didn't tell you with words, I'm sure you read my thoughts that evening when I couldn't stop drinking or crying.

Hold on to our secrets, our scenes onstage and in rooms, hold on to all the drinks we swilled and the tongues we sucked on. Hold on to our flair for dancing and getting a kick out of things that make a whole nation of weasels weep, a land doomed to neocolonial turmoil, the untouchability of a statue standing at the end of Humboldt, the monument that got us so wet because it was a landscape, that turned us on as much as seeing two men feeling up Mayuli. Hold on to me.

My memories are too precise. I know you find this boring, I know you think I've become boring. Things could've been different, of course they could've—less lewd, more pristine, with less blood, shit, piss, and drool in everything, less crap in our arteries. Things could've been different, but this is how they turned out, and the person who suffered more than anyone was never at the center of this story: Mayuli, I'm always thinking of Mayuli.

I will tell you about my scars, I will tell you about the lovers I never had, I will tell you about my hair, I will tell you about turning my back on costume design and theater, or maybe I'll tell you about a clothing store Jara and I opened in La Habana Vieja. I will tell you about how I failed. A famous photographer published a picture of us. Did you see the exhibition catalog? Our moment passed so quickly! Within a week, there were already two other girls exactly like us doing the same kind of theater. A new theater. Within a week, there was already another Mayuli, and those three people spent their time dying in meaningless places like the sports field of an abandoned school or on the roof of a condemned building or on a balcony with views of the Malecón.

Here, the weasels change convulsively. I don't know if I'm older or more fed up or just more bored than ever, but I wanted to write to you about our rose-colored years. Don't forget me, don't forget our toes playing on the balcony, don't forget the hunger we felt, our thirst for something cold, something hard, something so, so soft.

I'll tell you that I haven't forgotten you, I still read you on the balcony and still quit smoking every year, still fail at all my habits, good and bad. I fail, Pamela, the imaginary weasel sinks his teeth into me. I am an insect, a cockroach.

The air is thick, the people more disfigured, more engineered. We were two well-constructed girls, don't you think? We were exactly what you'd expect from a pair of artists in an inhospitable part of the planet. I have to confess: I'm writing to justify the ludicrousness of our age. You and I both know that all the parties and perspiration we lived through were just our ludicrous rebellions, our little battles, our own glorious cataclysm.

Did you fall in love like I did? I'll always remember how we went to Santa Clara and rode the carousel and you fell because you were crazy drunk and in love with a deaf-mute violinist. Maybe I've fabricated this memory, but I'm still going to tell it to you like it's real, and for sure it'll be the memory, the only memory that will make you think of us happy and in love.

Jara and I are in love, in love with our snow on the archipelago joined up by glaciers that floated up out of nowhere, and they changed the air and the misery of that little room in Centro Habana with the same family photos. You hate me with a passion when I tell you about my love, you remember how indifferent I seemed when Mayuli was imprisoned, you remember that if I can't love, then I'm just like the thing I despise more than anything, I'm just another weasel.

Did I ever tell you I got pregnant? I guess another thing I didn't tell you is that I slept with Mayuli. The reason I didn't tell you is that you didn't tell me you'd been with him too. You can't be a politician or a revolutionary with so much shit and girlfriends and flesh on the mind, you can't be a rebel with so much luxury, you can't stop history with so much fear and suffering.

I will never again use these words: censorship, dictatorship, police, theater, weasel. Ever. I'll tell you about my last orgasm, my most intense orgasm. She used this little battery-powered contraption and her tongue and all her tentacles. She put headphones over my ears, and I listened to these audio recordings that I can't even explain, all I can say is they're sad. It was short, cutting, like being stabbed with a knife. I'm happy, I swear, sometimes I'm happy with her.

Where are you reading this letter? Are you reading it aloud or to yourself? Are you rewriting it, like a good judgmental, cynical playwright?

I'll tell you about the silence of the small hours, of the closed dance clubs, of the claustrophobia I've felt since you left. I'll tell you about the design store I bulldozed into ruins. The weasels quickly gathered around and settled on the fabric and the tags in our shop in La Habana Vieja. I will tell you this "girly" story, a story about two women in love—angsty like a rebellious teen, older and more cancerous than a play.

I'm picturing you with blond hair. Did you dye it? It's so hard dyeing your hair platinum in this climate. I've never had smelly armpits again or dyed my hair extravagant colors.

Jara is trying to get pregnant. We've moved to an apartment in Vedado, and we're leasing out a small room in the back under the table and using that money to pay some of our bills. When the baby's born, that room will be the nursery. Jara's baby will be our baby. Deep down, I will always know that I'm dried up, knocked out by a tea that poisoned every inch of me, by the fictional child I never had.

You probably already have two blond kids, you were always going on about blond kids. I scribble your name in every drawing, just for the ritual of it, just to invoke your fondness for pretty things. Putting your name down on paper changes everything.

Sometimes I think I'm overly fixated on stuff that's dying, sometimes I think I'm the one killing things slowly, like those imaginary islands where I see myself, like our life together.

Do you want to come visit? I don't know if you'll get here in time for the cataclysm, for the open stores in peak tourist season, for you to visit our crumbling shop, for you to stay in my mother's room, for my throat cancer, for the shuttered theater, for the Sundays when I was raped.

My sister will be studying in London after getting a very important grant. My sister will graduate and stay on in the United Kingdom, and our mother will visit her a total of three times. I think my mother has always known that happiness means living for yourself, that ecosystems are made up, that the only real thing in the world is epilepsy.

I'm writing you with dried-up eardrums, with an echo, a void, a tonal abyss. Do you remember the night Fidel died?

Do you remember the Muestra de Cine Joven party? That night something inside me shattered, something grabbed hold of my arm and shoved me against the floor and dragged me to a high-school bathroom and made me think of a common rape, mass rape, gang rape. I never told you I was good, we were terrible, we were corny as hell, we were pure fad in a country behind the times, behind the world, behind the dreams of its own people.

Our clones don't realize they're clones. We the clones did not accept this, we looked down our noses at the lives of people in the cloned city, they are our replacements. The eldest weasels know full well that they are weasels. In my ears, the sound of a dying animal. That animal is me, that animal is my mother in the grips of a seizure, that animal is your tongue in my ear washing away the pain, washing away the pain of time. I'll tell you about freedom. I'll tell you about my French diet. I'll tell you about my savings and about our plan to take an "all-inclusive" trip.

I came out unscathed. They didn't even file a criminal charge against me. I was mixed up in something that surpassed my childlike criminal instincts. I was mixed up in shit, and the worst thing is it wasn't even for a good cause, I was like the respectful prostitute, a character with compromised-seeming morals and a heart of gold.

I'd never considered writing you this letter, I'd never considered telling you these fake, costumbrista vignettes. Laugh at me all you want, laugh from your belly and swear you won't write back. I've got *Elephant Family* and a play about my mother's career and political vocation.

THE WEASEL AND THE WHORE

I feel like I recognize you less and less in these songs. Will you come?

Sleeping in your arms and weeping. Walking together and saying hello to a bunch of strangers. Letting some pansies at Humboldt steal our phones. Living this weaselly life, living it comfortably and with a warm joy. I'll tell you about how I listen to track 7—so mortifying—and about how I'm writing a subversive novel about our life.

Pee your pants laughing, pee your pants laughing and promise it won't happen again: that our clones won't be so stuck, that they'll have fewer half-sunken mattresses, fewer ravenous wolves, less dark drool. I don't know if my mother will survive another seizure, if this big fat lie I've told you actually happened; at the end of the day it doesn't matter when a weasel has fabricated a truth that isn't real life.

Everything is still immutable. My rebellion in the body of a high-school friend who killed himself. My friend threw himself in front of a bus, and they couldn't put his body back together again. My friend was crushed by a cement water tank that also shattered his skull. My friend was murdered and dumped in a cistern. My friend was raped and chopped into pieces. My friend was a dog in a dogfight. My friend was biological refuse at a dumping site in the city center. My friend stabbed his aorta. My friend was a woman.

Go on, pee yourself a little, just like my mother, except you can do it joyfully—she'll do it because she'll die instantly. I imagine that I'm the one carrying Jara's child and pee myself a little. And with this piss I say goodbye to you. You've probably forgotten everything we've loved, everything we've wept for.

It feels like everything might just be alright today, that despite everything, today could be a great day. Today, there's chocolate ripple ice cream at Coppelia.

Love you, Mary

 MUNKEN

Learn more about the paper we use:

www.arcticpaper.com

Arctic Paper UK Ltd
8 St Thomas Street
London
SE1 9RS